TEACHER'S PET

Morris Gleitzman was born and educated in England. He went to Australia with his family in 1969 and studied for a degree. In 1974 he began work with ABC, left to become a full-time film and television writer in 1978 and has written numerous television scripts. He has two children and lives in Melbourne, but visits England regularly. Now one of the best-selling children's authors in Australia, his first children's book was *The Other Facts of Life*, based on his award-winning screenplay. This was followed by the highly acclaimed *Two Weeks with the Queen*, and he has since written many other books for children including *Toad Rage* and *Bumface,* and *Totally Wicked!* and *Deadly!* with Paul Jennings.

Visit Morris at his web site:
www.morrisgleitzman.com

Books by Morris Gleitzman

TEACHER'S PET

THE OTHER FACTS OF LIFE

SECOND CHILDHOOD

TWO WEEKS WITH THE QUEEN

MISERY GUTS

WORRY WARTS

PUPPY FAT

BLABBER MOUTH

STICKY BEAK

GIFT OF THE GAB

BELLY FLOP

WATER WINGS

BUMFACE

ADULTS ONLY

TOAD RAGE

TOAD HEAVEN

BOY OVERBOARD

Books by Morris Gleitzman with Paul Jennings

DEADLY!

TOTALLY WICKED!

Morris GLEITZMAN

Teacher's Pet

PUFFIN

PUFFIN BOOKS

Published by the Penguin Group
Penguin Books Ltd, 80 Strand, London WC2R 0RL, England
Penguin Putnam Inc., 375 Hudson Street, New York, New York 10014, USA
Penguin Books Australia Ltd, 250 Camberwell Road, Camberwell, Victoria 3124, Australia
Penguin Books Canada Ltd, 10 Alcorn Avenue, Toronto, Ontario, Canada M4V 3B2
Penguin Books India (P) Ltd, 11 Community Centre, Panchsheel Park, New Delhi – 110 017, India
Penguin Books (NZ) Ltd, Cnr Rosedale and Airborne Roads, Albany, Auckland, New Zealand
Penguin Books (South Africa) (Pty) Ltd, 24 Sturdee Avenue, Rosebank 2196, South Africa

Penguin Books Ltd, Registered Offices: 80 Strand, London WC2R 0RL, England

www.penguin.com

First published in Australia by Penguin Books Australia 2003
Published in Great Britain in Puffin Books 2004
8

Made and printed in England by Clays Ltd, St Ives plc

British Library Cataloguing in Publication Data
A CIP catalogue record for this book is available from the British Library

ISBN 0–141–31755–8
ISBN-13: 978–0–14–131755–7

www.greenpenguin.co.uk

For
Tom, Harry, Bridget, Kim, Ellen, Joe, Isabel,
Edward, Jack, Jamie, Phillipa, Bethany,
Prudence, George, Harriet, Billy and Charlie.

1

BEWARE OF THE DOG

Something didn't smell right.

Ginger stopped halfway down Ashmore Street and sniffed the air.

Her nose tingled.

Her insides tightened.

Was it?

She couldn't be sure.

All the normal walking-to-school smells were there. The soft tang of carports warming up in the sun. The faint but exotic fragrance of mums and dads frying breakfast for their kids. The lovely minty aroma of families cleaning their teeth and telling each other jokes and laughing and spraying toothpaste around the bathroom.

Ginger sighed and tried not to feel jealous.

She could still smell something else.

Something not right.

I'm going to ignore it, Ginger decided. I'm not going to let it spoil my day.

She turned her walkman up, headed along the street and concentrated on making up swearwords for her school assignment.

Suddenly Ginger's nose went mental, tingling so hard her eyes watered.

It was.

The smell was exactly what she'd feared.

A cat.

Oh fuguggle, she thought, screwing up her nose.

She sneezed. A big wet sneeze that made her stagger and almost drop both schoolbags and fall off the kerb.

Embarrassed, Ginger squinted around to see if she'd sprayed anyone. Luckily the street was almost deserted. But not quite. A car went past and Ginger was pretty sure it had its windscreen wipers on.

'Sorry,' she said.

A fuguggling cat, she thought as she got ready to sneeze again. That's all I fuguggling need.

It was bad enough Mum and Dad rushing off to a meeting without asking a person if she needed a lift to school. Leaving a person to lug her little sister's left-behind schoolbag. But finding a cat had invaded your one cat-free way to school was enough to make you weep.

Ginger sneezed instead.

It was another big one and it nearly flipped her walkman headphones out of her ears.

She wiped away the sneeze tears and peered up and down the street, trying to see if the cat was a sneaky tabby or a snooty know-it-all Siamese or one of those explosions of fluff that look like they've had gunpowder up their bum.

Nothing.

Not a cat to be seen.

Just a dog.

A big shaggy dog, standing across the street, staring at her.

Ginger stared back.

She could see it wasn't wearing a collar. She always felt sad when she saw dogs like that. Poor mutts without anyone to care for them.

Abandoned.

Forgotten.

Probably a victim of workaholic parents, thought Ginger. She gave the dog a sympathetic smile.

Then she felt several more sneezes starting.

Fuguggling great, she thought. Now I'm allergic to dogs too.

After Ginger finished sneezing, she pulled herself out of the hedge she'd fallen into, slung the school-bags over her shoulders again and staggered down the street towards school.

Her nose ached.

She hoped the cat was behind her and not hiding up ahead, planning an ambush. She'd read somewhere that repeated sneezing while you're weighed down with two schoolbags could damage your spine.

She glanced across the road.

The dog was walking along on the other side of the street, keeping up with her.

Still staring.

What a weird dog, thought Ginger.

It looked like a cross between a shaggy Eskimo dog and an overgrown cattle dog, except it was black.

Ginger wondered how a stray dog without a family to groom it or give it marrowbone jelly could stay looking so glossy. By spending hours licking its fur, probably, so people wouldn't spot it was a stray and chuck things at it.

The thought made Ginger's eyes prickle, and she knew it wasn't a sneeze starting.

She stopped and turned her music down.

The dog stopped too.

'G'day,' said Ginger, giving it a friendly smile.

The dog bared its teeth. Ginger saw how big they were and how sharp. But for some reason they didn't look scary. Perhaps it was because of the puzzled glint in the dog's eyes.

Poor thing's probably confused, she thought. Probably used to people saying g'day with rocks.

'Sorry I can't stop and play,' she said. 'You know what it's like. Parents with busy careers. Plus I have a very forgetful little sister. I've got to keep moving so I can get to school before my shoulders fall off.'

Ginger pointed to the bags. The dog looked like it understood. Almost like it felt sorry for her.

4

Suddenly Ginger wished people would be kinder to animals.

Well, some animals.

'You can walk with me if you like,' she said, setting off again.

Across the street the dog trotted along, keeping level with her.

I bet it's hungry, thought Ginger. She wished she could do something to help. But what? It was hard to think with the bags thumping her in the hips and her neck killing her and only five minutes till the bell.

Then Ginger had an idea.

Mitzi's lunch.

If you have to carry your sister's bag, thought Ginger, you should be allowed to share her lunch. Specially as she never finishes it.

'Do you like Vegemite and fishfinger sandwiches?' Ginger asked the dog.

As far as she could see, the dog wasn't screwing up its face or gagging.

'Good,' said Ginger. 'I've got some breakfast for you.'

Without stopping, she stuffed her headphones into her pocket and tried to unzip Mitzi's bag. She couldn't because the bag was swinging about on her shoulder so much. She stopped to make it easier.

The bag kept moving.

Ginger stared at it.

Something was moving inside the bag.

Oh no, she begged silently. Please no.

Another big sneeze said yes.

Ginger regained her balance, wiped her face and unzipped Mitzi's bag, just a fraction. She peeped in. And saw exactly what she'd dreaded she'd see.

A pair of accusing eyes. A bunch of indignant whiskers. All surrounded by very irate orange fur.

Ginger wrenched the zip shut and sneezed again.

She felt faint. No wonder Mitzi's bag was so heavy. It wasn't overdue library books in there, it was Cornflake.

Why would anyone put a cat in their schoolbag?

Suddenly, as Cornflake started meowing loudly and crossly, Ginger remembered why.

School Pets Day.

Ginger was seized by the desire to yell so loudly that Mitzi would hear her all the way down the road in school.

Pets Day, she wanted to yell, isn't till next Thursday.

Ginger was halfway through planning the type of diary she was going to buy Mitzi, and the type of torture she was going to invent to make Mitzi use it, when she remembered the dog.

The dog must have stopped when she had. It was still staring at her from across the street, eyes glinting, not looking at all worried by the amount of saliva and snot that had been flying around.

Its ears had pricked up.

In the bag, Cornflake's muffled complaints were getting even louder.

Oh fuguggle, thought Ginger. I've just offered breakfast to a starving stray dog and it thinks I mean Cornflake.

Now the dog's teeth did look scary.

Ginger wondered if she should try and explain to the dog that it was all a mistake. That it wouldn't be fair to attack a person who only had a cat on them by accident.

She decided not to.

The dog wasn't standing still any more, it was moving across the street, coming at her, its breath rasping out through its fearsome teeth.

Pausing only to sneeze two more times, Ginger grabbed the bags and ran.

2

CAT OUT OF THE BAG

'Look out,' yelled Ginger. 'Savage dog.'

On the school crossing, Rita the lollipop lady's eyes went wide with alarm.

Ginger grabbed Rita and dragged her in through the school gate. She'd never dragged an adult before. They were really heavy.

'Quick,' panted Ginger once they were both inside.

She dumped the schoolbags and hurled herself at the gate, struggling to push it shut before fifty kilos of killer mongrel burst through and started eating kids.

The gate was stiff and Ginger could hardly move it. She wondered why Rita wasn't helping. Poor thing must be frozen with fear.

Isabel appeared at Ginger's side, pushing too.

Ginger said a silent prayer of thanks for best friends, specially short ones with strong arms.

'Why are we closing the gate?' asked Isabel.

'Savage dog,' said Ginger.

The gate clicked shut, and Ginger braced herself against it in case the latch wasn't up to the impact when the dog slammed into it.

Except there wasn't any impact.

'What savage dog?' asked Isabel.

Ginger peered through the bars of the gate.

The dog had vanished.

'It was a big black one,' said Ginger. 'Wasn't it, Rita?'

Rita lowered her lollipop and gave an awkward shrug. 'I didn't actually see it in the flesh,' she said. 'But if there was a savage dog you did the right thing, Ginger. Yelling to scare it away. Good yelling, too. Scared all of us.'

Ginger saw that everyone in the playground was staring at her. Locklan Grosby was frozen halfway through giving Ned Timms a wedgie. A group of Year Three girls were motionless in mid-skip, their ropes dangling.

'There was a dog,' said Ginger, trembling partly from shock and partly because she could see some people didn't believe her. 'I thought it was going to get me.'

Mrs Kalinski from the tuckshop patted Ginger's arm with a hand that smelled of anti-bacterial kitchen wipes and mini-pizzas.

'You poor love,' she said. 'I don't like dogs much either. Except for poodles.'

Ms Cunningham, the new teacher-librarian, took

9

off her leather jacket and put it round Ginger's shoulders.

'You were very brave,' she said. 'Dogs can be very vicious. I've seen what they can do to library books.'

Bruno the handyman, pausing in the middle of marking up the playground for Pets Day, brandished his leaf-blower.

'If the mongrel comes back,' he said, 'I'll blast it.'

Ginger started to feel better.

'What's going on?' said a voice.

Ginger turned, and didn't feel better any more.

Mr Napier, the assistant principal, was striding towards her. He had a smile on his face. Ginger's insides turned to kitty litter. She knew what that smile meant.

Trouble.

'Savage dog went for Ginger,' said Rita. 'We repelled it, but. If I see it again I'll give it a whack with my lollipop.'

Mr Napier peered out through the gate. Then he opened it and looked up and down the street.

There was still no sign of the dog.

Ginger felt like a total prawn.

Mr Napier shook his head with the same long-suffering expression Mum got when one of the cats was sick in her shoes.

'This savage dog,' he said. 'That wouldn't be it there, would it, in your bag?'

Ginger's stomach turned, and it wasn't just because of Mr Napier's chemical aftershave.

Mr Napier was pointing at Mitzi's bag, which was writhing around at Ginger's feet.

Some of the kids in the playground were laughing. Mr Napier grinned and winked at them as if he was in their gang, which Ginger thought was a bit pathetic at his age.

'Well,' said Mr Napier to Ginger. 'Is that the savage dog?'

'No,' said Ginger helplessly.

She could see Mr Napier didn't believe her. He turned to the kids in the playground, raised his eyebrows in a show-off way, then turned back to Ginger.

'What is it then?' he demanded. 'A cat?'

The kids in the playground all thought this was hilarious.

Ginger didn't say anything. She saw Isabel's eyes widen with concern and she knew that Isabel had just realised it probably was a cat.

'Let's take a look, shall we?' Mr Napier said to the kids in the playground.

He grinned at them again, then bent down and started to unzip Mitzi's bag.

Ginger stepped forward to warn him, but it was too late. A hissing bundle of orange fury exploded out of the bag and attached itself to Mr Napier's head.

Ginger gasped.

Then she sneezed.

Mr Napier screamed. The long piece of hair he combed over his bald patch had slid off his scalp and was dangling past one ear with Cornflake hanging off the end.

The kids in the playground howled even louder. Rita joined in. Mr Napier shook his head violently. Cornflake hung on.

Ginger watched Cornflake being tossed around like a ball of fluff at a funfair.

Let go, you stupid cat, she advised Cornflake silently.

Finally Mr Napier grabbed Cornflake, tore her off his hair and flung her to the ground. Cornflake gave everyone an angry look, then bolted into the Year Five Sculpture Garden.

Mr Napier gave the kids in the playground an even angrier look. They stopped laughing immediately.

When Rita realised she was the only one still laughing, she stopped too.

Mr Napier replaced his hair across his scalp, then turned to Ginger.

She tried to look him in the eye so he could see it wasn't her fault even though she couldn't actually say so. It wasn't easy. The one thing scarier than Mr Napier smiling was when he wasn't.

Mr Napier put his hand in his pocket, took out a tissue, bent towards Ginger and wiped her nose.

Ginger blushed. It had been a stringy sneeze.

'I pity your parents,' said Mr Napier, glaring at Ginger. 'Go and find that cat. I want to see you, and it, in my office.'

He turned and walked away across the playground.

'Dropkick,' muttered Rita, scowling at him.

'You should have told him it was Mitzi's bag,' said Isabel.

Ginger sighed. Isabel was an only kid, so she couldn't be expected to know that you never dob on your own family, even if sometimes they don't feel very much like your family.

Mrs Kalinski and Ms Cunningham were already off looking for Cornflake, and Ginger was about to join them when she heard a desperate shout.

'Ginger. Ginger. Quick.'

It was Mitzi, running over from the carpark, hair bunches flapping, waving her arms like a monkey puppet.

'Ginger,' she gasped. 'I forgot my bag. Cornflake's in it. Mum and Dad said you have to go back and …'

Mitzi saw her bag on the ground and stopped. She picked it up and looked inside. Her face crumpled in anguish.

'Cornflake,' she wailed. 'Where's Cornflake?'

Ginger felt her insides soften and suddenly she wanted to put her arms round Mitzi.

Before she could, Isabel swore. 'Oh shiddlepong,' she said. 'I hope the cat doesn't run into that shiddleponging dog.'

Ginger gave Isabel a look. You're my best friend, the look said, but shut the fuguggle up, you're scaring my sister.

'Cornflake's lost,' sobbed Mitzi.

Ginger gave her a hug.

'Don't worry,' she said. 'I'll find your cat.'

Ginger stood in the school office, desperate.

She'd looked everywhere. The tuckshop, the library, the toilets, all the classrooms, even under the table-tennis table in the staff room.

Cornflake had vanished.

Mrs Aljon was Ginger's last hope.

'What was the cat's name again, dear?' said Mrs Aljon.

'Cornflake,' said Ginger.

Mrs Aljon spoke into the microphone. 'Cornflake to the office please,' she said. 'Would Cornflake please come to the office.'

Ginger sighed. Mrs Aljon obviously didn't know much about cats.

'Please,' said Ginger. 'Can I?'

She squeezed past Mrs Aljon and grabbed the microphone.

'Attention everyone,' she said. 'If anyone's found a cat in the last twenty minutes, please bring it to the office as quickly as possible and don't let it go anywhere near Mr Napier's head.'

Ginger took a deep breath to repeat the message, but before she was able to, a voice snapped out behind her.

'Step away from that microphone.'

Ginger turned.

Oh fuguggle.

Mr Napier was glaring at her from the doorway.

'It's all right, Mr Napier,' stammered Mrs Aljon. 'Ginger was just helping me because I was … I was …'

Mr Napier ignored her.

'You know the rule,' he said to Ginger. 'Students are forbidden to use the public address system without permission from either myself or the principal.'

Ginger found her voice again. 'But you told me to find Cornflake.'

Mr Napier sighed. He moved towards her. Ginger saw he had about six Band-aids on his head. She felt a bit guilty about that.

'Ginger, Ginger, Ginger,' said Mr Napier. 'Sometimes I despair about you. How did a nice family like yours end up with a person like you in it?'

Ginger stared at him. What did he mean? The minty fumes of his mouthwash were making her gag. She didn't bother replying because she could see he hadn't finished.

Mr Napier crouched close to her and frowned as if he was about to tell her a very sad secret.

'I've heard people around here saying,' he whispered, 'that when you were born, there must have been a mix-up at the hospital. Your parents must have taken the wrong baby home.'

Ginger scowled at him.

'Do you think that's possible?' asked Mr Napier.

No, thought Ginger. I don't.

Plus she couldn't think of a single person in the school who'd say that. Except Locklan Grosby, but he didn't have the imagination.

Ginger struggled with a powerful urge to bite Mr Napier on the leg.

'What I hope,' said Mr Napier, 'is that you can prove us all wrong. Show us you do belong in that family. Starting with not leaving your bag lying around.'

Mr Napier picked Ginger's bag up off the floor and thrust it under her chin.

Ginger couldn't stay quiet any longer. She opened her mouth to say that there hadn't been a mix-up at the hospital and that she had the photos to prove it.

But the words didn't come out, just a huge sneeze.

A very stringy one.

Right into Mr Napier's face.

Ginger couldn't see all the details because her eyes were full of sneeze tears, but she could imagine and it was pretty horrible.

'Sorry,' she gasped.

Some of Cornflake's hairs must be near by. In her bag. Or stuck to Mr Napier's Band-aids.

When Ginger's eyes cleared, she saw Mr Napier was wiping his face with his hanky. She couldn't see his expression, but she could guess what it looked like from the fury in his voice.

'Quite obviously,' he said, 'you have a serious medical condition. Go to the sickroom while I decide what to do with you. I think there's a teacher tidying up in there. Tell that teacher exactly why I've sent you.'

Ginger turned to leave the office. She hoped the teacher in the sickroom was someone who would understand. Then she saw that behind the filing cabinet Mrs Aljon was winking at her and giving her a thumbs-up.

Ginger's insides went into a tight and painful furball.

Oh no.

Not that teacher.

3

WET NOSES

Ginger tapped miserably on the sickroom door.

While she was waiting for it to open, a little kid holding a bunch of bloodstained tissues to his nose came and stood next to her.

'Is Mrs Smith in there?' he asked Ginger.

I hope not, thought Ginger.

'Don't know,' she said. 'Tilt your head forward.'

The door opened.

A familiar face looked down at them.

'Mrs Smith,' said the little kid, 'I've got a nosebleed.'

'Excuse me,' said Ginger to the kid. 'I was first.'

She turned back to the teacher.

'Mum,' she said, 'it's not fair. Mitzi accidentally put Cornflake in her bag and I sneezed on Mr Napier and he's blaming me for …'

Mum interrupted her.

'Ginger,' she said wearily. 'We've been through this a million times. At school I'm Mrs Smith,

18

remember? Now be patient, pet. I think this young man needs me.'

Ginger gritted her teeth.

Mum turned to the little kid and Ginger watched Mum's face soften with concern.

'Come on, you poor love,' said Mum. 'Let's get some ice on that.'

As Mum put her arm round the kid's shoulders and started to steer him into the room, another teacher came along the corridor.

'Brian,' said Mum, 'could you give me a hand with this?'

Ginger watched the other teacher peer at the little kid and hurry over, making sympathetic noises.

'Dad,' said Ginger. 'I mean Mr Smith, it's not fair …'

'Hold that thought,' said Dad, following Mum and the kid into the sickroom. 'We've got a bit of an emergency here. Stay put and one of us will see you in a bit, OK pet?'

He closed the door.

Ginger's teeth were so gritted her jaw ached.

She thought of the number of times other kids had told her how lucky she was to have her mum and dad teaching at the school.

They usually said it after Mum and Dad had helped them with their homework or got their bags down from trees or given them lemonade after they'd drunk paintbrush water for a dare. There was always a queue of kids wanting Mum and Dad.

With me, thought Ginger sadly, always at the end of it.

While Ginger waited in the corridor, she tried not to think about any tragic but likely cat disasters that might have happened.

Cornflake squashed flat under a bus, for example. Or Cornflake in the jaws of the killer dog. Or Cornflake in the music room trying to get the cassette player to work and sticking her paw in a power socket and electrocuting herself.

And Mitzi sobbing her little heart out.

Ginger closed her eyes and took a deep breath.

School smells always calmed her down.

Then she heard voices coming towards her along the corridor. She opened her eyes. It was Locklan Grosby and some of the other boys from class.

Ginger waited for Locklan to greet her with his usual hilarious crack about Sneezy Smith. He didn't. He was too busy giving Ned Timms a hard time.

'Hey, Neddy,' Locklan was saying. 'I reckon Pets Day's really cruel, eh?'

Ginger could see that Ned was wishing he was somewhere else.

'Not if everyone looks after their pets,' he mumbled.

'I don't mean cruel to animals,' said Locklan, grinning at his mates. 'I mean cruel to people like you who haven't got a pet.'

The other boys chuckled.

'I have got a pet,' said Ned miserably.

Ginger could see from his face he probably didn't. Families with as many kids as Ned's didn't usually have the food or the bowls to spare for pets.

'Like squill you've got a pet,' chortled Locklan. 'Like rinnock. Like squink. Like nurgly. Like krrrrk.'

Ginger rolled her eyes. Locklan was the sort of kid who, when everyone was asked to invent a swearword for an assignment, had to invent six.

'OK, what is your pet?' said Locklan to Ned. 'An ant? A spider? A squinking headlice?'

The other boys cracked up. Ginger didn't even smile. She saw the hurt on Ned's long horsey face as he went past.

Stupid fuguggles, she thought. Why can't they just stop picking on Ned? Let him be in their gang. That's all he wants. It's not much to ask.

Suddenly Ginger found herself running after the boys.

'G'day Ned,' she said loudly. 'How's Killer?'

The boys all stared at her. Ned looked confused.

'Who the squink's Killer?' asked Locklan, pink with aggro.

What am I doing? Ginger asked herself in silent panic.

She looked Locklan square in the eyes.

'Ned's pet,' she said. 'You must have seen Killer. Giant Peruvian tree spider. It's won heaps of pet shows, even with its muzzle on. You'd better watch out on Pets Day, Locklan, or it'll eat that fuguggling dog of yours for playlunch.'

Ginger saw a smile breaking out on Ned's face.

'How big is it?' demanded Locklan uncertainly.

'I'm not allowed to say,' said Ned. 'It's too illegal. If the police catch it they'll put it in the poonwoggling zoo.'

Ginger swapped a grin with Ned.

He looked so grateful she wanted to hug him.

Sometimes school could be really good.

Ginger hurried back to the sickroom.

She didn't make it.

'Ginger Smith,' hissed Mr Napier, stepping out of his office. 'I sent you to the sickroom. What are you doing wandering around the corridor?'

Ginger tried to swallow but her mouth was too dry. She opened it to see what answer came out, but Mr Napier didn't want an answer.

He gave such a big sigh that several of the Band-aids on his head crinkled.

'Ginger, Ginger, Ginger,' he said. 'What are we going to do with you?'

How about hanging a big sign round my neck, thought Ginger. Mr And Mrs Smith. This Is Your Daughter. Please Spare Her A Few Minutes.

Ginger didn't suggest this because Mr Napier wouldn't understand.

Or that's what she thought.

'You poor thing,' said Mr Napier, shaking his head. 'It must be awful, having your parents here all day. Having to share them with all the other kids.'

Ginger stared at him.

Incredible. He understood. Could this be the same Mr Napier who'd been mean to her ever since he'd arrived at the school six months ago?

Perhaps she'd got him wrong. Perhaps underneath he was a loving husband and father. Ginger tried to remember hearing Mum or Dad mention Mr Napier's wife and kids. The only name that sprang to mind was Corolla, but she was pretty sure that was his car.

Mr Napier was looking at her, frowning.

'What I don't understand,' he said, 'is why having your parents here doesn't affect your sister in the same way. She doesn't lie and disobey and break school rules.'

Ginger's mouth was starting to feel dry again. This was beginning to sound more like the Mr Napier she knew and sometimes had bad dreams about.

'Mitzi likes cats,' she said. 'They help her cope.'

Mr Napier sighed again. On his breath Ginger could smell onions and stale lollies.

'Well,' said Mr Napier, 'let's see if we can find a way of helping you cope.'

For a fleeting moment Ginger wondered if he'd think of hanging a sign round her neck too.

'In fact,' continued Mr Napier, 'I'm thinking

I may have found a way. What if I see if I can get you transferred to another school?'

Ginger struggled to take in what he'd just said.

Another school?

She felt like she'd been slapped round the face with a wet cat. She desperately tried to find the words to tell Mr Napier she didn't want to be sent away, to explain that all the people she cared about in the world were at this school, to promise she'd try harder.

Instead she sneezed.

She caught it just in time, pulling up the front of her windcheater and burying her nose in it and muffling the explosion and the snot.

That was close, she thought weakly.

If she'd given Mr Napier a second faceful she'd have been in another school by lunchtime.

'Bless you,' said a voice behind Ginger.

She turned, blinking away the tears.

It was Mr Wong, the principal. Purring happily in his arms was Cornflake.

'I think this runaway belongs to you,' said Mr Wong to Ginger, beaming. When Mr Wong smiled, all his wrinkles joined in. He didn't look even a tiny bit upset about having cat hair on his cardigan.

Ginger tried to thank Mr Wong, but her voice was still in shock.

Cornflake gave Ginger a glare.

Ginger, struggling not to sneeze again, glanced

anxiously at Mr Napier, waiting for him to tell Mr Wong about having her transferred. She knew Mr Wong wouldn't like the idea. But Mum reckoned he often took Mr Napier's advice. Dad reckoned it was because Mr Napier had a university degree in school management.

Mr Napier pulled out his hanky and wiped the snot off Ginger's windcheater.

'I was just explaining something to Ginger here,' he said to Mr Wong. 'How pets are only allowed at school on Pets Day itself. And how vicious animals like this one aren't welcome at all.'

Mr Wong tickled Cornflake behind the ears. Ginger wondered if she should warn Mr Wong that Cornflake might look cute, but she was still a cat.

'This one's not vicious,' said Mr Wong. 'Cheeky perhaps, and a bit headstrong, but intelligent, honest and very likeable. Quite like her owner in fact.'

He smiled at Ginger.

Mr Napier smiled too, but Ginger saw that his eyes were slits, like a constipated cat's.

'Actually,' said Ginger to Mr Wong, 'Cornflake belongs to my sister.'

This seemed to amuse Mr Wong. He gave Ginger an even bigger smile.

'The fact remains,' broke in Mr Napier, 'that today is not Pets Day.'

'I know,' said Mr Wong. Suddenly he looked very tired. 'We've had twenty-three annual Pets Days at this school and we've had a child and a pet getting the day wrong at least, oh, twenty-three times.' He patted Mr Napier on the shoulder. 'You'll get used to it when you've been here a couple more years.'

Mr Napier didn't look to Ginger like he'd get used to it even if he was there a couple more centuries.

'Here,' said Mr Wong, holding Cornflake out to Ginger.

Cornflake stiffened and stopped purring.

Ginger struggled not to sneeze.

'Actually,' she said, 'would you be able to give her directly to my sister?'

Mr Wong nodded again and Ginger could see he understood.

'I think perhaps we should give her to your parents to look after,' he said. 'Come on, Ginger, you lead the way.'

Ginger hurried away with Mr Wong, not looking back. She heard Mr Napier clear his throat and call after them.

'Mr Wong, can I see you in your office in ten minutes? There's something I want to discuss with you.'

'Righty-o,' said Mr Wong.

Ginger's stomach suddenly felt like it was full of the stuff cats threw up when they'd been eating grass.

She knew exactly what Mr Napier wanted to discuss.

4

HOUNDING MUM AND DAD

Ginger sneezed and sprayed pasta sauce across the dinner table.

Fuguggle, she thought bitterly. This always happens when I've got something important to tell people. A cat muscles in and I end up losing everyone's attention because of the flying snot and bits of tomato.

'Pet,' said Mum. 'Try not to sneeze while we're eating.'

'Cover your face, pet,' said Dad.

'Yuk,' said Mitzi.

'I can't help it,' said Ginger, picking up Ricebubble and dropping her onto the floor. 'She jumped onto my lap.'

Mum gave a big sigh.

'Ginger,' she said. 'Don't blame the poor cats. We've been through this a million times. You don't know for sure it's the cats you're allergic to. It could be dust or pot plants or pasta or anything. It could even be stress after your terrible experience today with that dog.'

'Alice Burchill in my class,' said Mitzi, 'is allergic to car seat covers.'

'Exactly,' said Mum. 'When this term settles down and I'm not so busy, I'll take you for some more tests, pet.'

Ginger nodded sadly.

She wished Mum could be allergic to cats, just for half an hour, just in one nostril, so she'd know.

'Have you had a tablet?' asked Dad.

'Two,' said Ginger. 'They don't work when the cats or the pasta or the pot plants jump on me.'

'Don't be cheeky,' said Mum. 'The cats want to be on your lap because they're fond of you, pet.'

Ginger looked around the room. Cornflake and Ricebubble were in the sink, glaring at her, their long orange hair bristling with anger. The other three cats didn't look fond of her either, even though Isabel reckoned short-haired cats had nicer natures. Madonna was curled up in a pot plant, chewing something that was probably a flower. Kylie was sprawled on the coffee table watching TV with a bored expression. Cher was on the settee, frowning at the wall as if she'd never seen such daggy wallpaper.

Ginger sighed.

'I don't think they're fond of anyone,' she said.

Mum looked a bit hurt.

'They love us very deeply,' she said. 'We're their family.'

Something hard hit Ginger on the head. Pain meowed through her skull.

'Ow,' she said, rubbing herself.

On the table next to her plate she saw what had hit her.

A small china cat.

'Look out,' yelled Mitzi, pointing above Ginger's head.

Ginger looked up. Ricebubble had jumped up on a shelf and was sliding another china cat towards the edge with her paw.

Ginger stood up angrily.

'Ricebubble, naughty,' said Mum. 'Ginger, don't get cross. She just wants your attention. She's your special cat. You never spend any time with her.'

Runs in the family, thought Ginger as she grabbed Ricebubble off the shelf. She leaned down, dumped Ricebubble on the floor and sneezed so hard she banged her head on the table leg. Now Ginger's skull was throbbing twice as much.

'I didn't want a special cat,' she said to Mum and Dad. 'I just wanted a goldfish like Isabel's.'

Dad looked hurt.

Mum rolled her eyes. 'We've got a house full of cats, pet,' she said. 'It wouldn't have been fair on a goldfish.'

'It's not fuguggling fair on me,' yelled Ginger.

There was a silence.

Mitzi stared at her plate.

Mum squeezed her lips together.

'Fuguggling,' said Dad after a while. 'That's a good one.'

Ginger decided to put off asking for Mum and Dad's help till the morning. She was too upset now. Losing her temper always made her sneeze even more and if she tried to tell Mum and Dad about Mr Napier tonight, they'd probably end up cowering under the table with napkins on their heads.

Mum got up and came over and put her arms round Ginger.

'We're a family,' she said. 'You and me and Mitzi and Dad and Ricebubble and Cornflake and Cher and Kylie and Madonna. Families have their ups and downs but they get over them because they belong together. Right, pet?'

'Right,' said Ginger.

She gave Mum a very hard hug because she wanted it to be true.

She loved her family very deeply too, even though three of them were cat lovers and five of them were cats.

'Ginger,' yelled Mum. 'Hurry up. Mitzi's ready. You're making us late. I'm doing your breakfast. It's on the bench.'

Of course I'm making us late, thought Ginger as she hurried into the kitchen. What do you expect when I'm sneezing every two minutes? How can I be on time when there's a cat on my towel, a cat in the dirty washing basket and a cat eating the toothpaste?

She opened her mouth to say this to Mum, then closed it.

No point.

Mum was already Mrs Smith, dashing round the kitchen pouring Ginger's cereal and stuffing things in the dishwasher with one hand and reading a wad of school paperwork clutched in the other.

Ginger put a spoonful of cereal into her mouth and chewed sadly. Then she gagged, sneezed and sprayed the mouthful over the bench.

She stared at the soggy pieces in horror.

'Mum …' she groaned.

Before she could say anything else, Dad strode in, also with a fistful of paperwork.

'Look at this,' said Dad. 'The McKenzie parents have written to the school thanking us for that creative writing project I gave Year Six. The one where I asked them to make up new swearwords. They reckon it's the only project their kids have ever finished.'

'You're a tweetwobbling genius,' muttered Mum, still reading. 'Oh no, look at this, the Funicellos want to know if Lucrezia can bring a goat to Pets Day.'

Ginger decided to forget what had happened in the bathroom and with breakfast. She had something much more important to talk about before school started.

'Mum,' she said. 'Dad.'

They didn't even look up. They were both studying a sheet of paper and talking about Andy Malkovich's skin rash.

'Excuse me,' said Ginger loudly. 'Mr and Mrs Smith.'

They both looked up, startled.

Ginger didn't give them a chance to get distracted.

'Mr Napier reckons he's going to get me transferred,' she said. 'To another school.'

Ginger held her breath while Mum and Dad looked at each other.

Then they both put on their Mr and Mrs Smith faces.

'Ginger,' said Mum. 'I'm sure it's not that bad. Mr Napier can be a bit strict, but he's a reasonable man. You know how when teachers get overworked they sometimes say things they don't mean.'

'He does mean it,' said Ginger. 'You've got to talk to him.'

Dad gave a Mr Smith sigh.

'I'm sure Mr Napier was only joking,' he said. 'This is another of those tricky ones, Ginger. You know we can't interfere.'

'Why not?' said Ginger.

'You'll understand when you're a bit older,' said Mum. 'Teachers can't go around telling assistant principals how to do their jobs. Not unless it's about something really serious.'

'It is really serious,' yelled Ginger.

She turned away in frustration. Madonna and Cher were on top of the stove, watching her with disdain. She could see they didn't think that anything in her life was the slightest bit serious.

'We've discussed this before, pet,' said Mum quietly. 'We can't have people at school thinking we're giving our daughter special treatment.'

Fat chance, thought Ginger.

'Come on, girls,' said Dad. 'Into the car. Nobody's walking, not until the council does something about these stray dogs.'

Mum grabbed her briefcase from the kitchen bench, stopped and sighed. 'Pet, you haven't eaten your cereal. Why not?'

'Because,' said Ginger, pointing to the half-chewed prawn-flavoured fragments in the puddles of milk, 'it's cat food.'

Ginger felt better by the time she got to school.

In the car she'd had a really good thought. A thought she wished she'd had last night instead of lying awake worrying.

'Mr Napier's not the principal, he's only the assistant principal,' she said to Isabel in the play-ground. 'So even if he has got a university degree in being bossy, he can't transfer me unless Mr Wong agrees. Mr Wong might be a bit frail with age, but he believes in justice. I'll go and see Mr Wong and explain everything to him.'

Ginger stopped.

She could see Isabel wasn't paying attention.

Great, thought Ginger. I'm grappling with a crisis and my best friend's distracted by an empty plastic fish bowl.

Isabel was holding the bowl up to the sky and staring at it adoringly.

'Thanks, Ginger,' she said. 'Are you sure I can have this?'

'I bought it when I thought I was getting a goldfish,' said Ginger. 'When I was young and hopeful.'

'It'll be so shiddleponging good,' said Isabel, breathing on the bowl and polishing it with her windcheater. 'I could never have brought Finger to Pets Day in his big tank. Now I can bring him in this and he can meet other fish.'

'I'm glad,' said Ginger. 'So what do you reckon? About explaining everything to Mr Wong. Do you think he'll stop Mr Napier transferring me to another school?'

Isabel stared at her in alarm. 'Another school?'

Ginger sighed. Sometimes best friends had the attention spans of parents.

Isabel's face suddenly looked even more stricken and Ginger saw she'd just remembered something.

'Mr Wong can't help,' said Isabel. 'He's off sick.'

'Off sick?' said Ginger, insides plummeting.

'It happened when he was leaving school yesterday evening in the dark,' said Isabel. 'He got bitten on the foot by a dog. Lollipop Rita told me. They reckon it might have been the dog that chased you.'

Ginger's head spun as she took this in.

'Poor Mr Wong,' she said. 'How bad is he hurt?'

'Rita said she's not a doctor but she reckons he probably won't be back for a while.'

Ginger tried to get her thoughts in order. If Mr Wong was off sick, that meant somebody else would have to stand in as acting principal.

Mum could do it.

Or Dad.

They could do it together. They could save her from being sent away.

Then Ginger realised Isabel had grabbed her arm.

She saw from the panic on her friend's face that it wasn't Mum who was in charge now.

Or Dad.

Ginger felt panic get its claws into her too.

'Oh no,' she gasped. 'Not Mr Napier.'

5

CATASTROPHE

'This is a wonderful school,' said Mr Napier. 'And I'm very proud to be its acting principal.'

Ginger felt sick.

Mr Napier was looking down from the stage with a big smile on his face.

From her assembly monitor position at the side of the hall, Ginger could see that out of about twenty rows of kids and teachers only about three people were smiling back.

Mr Napier paused.

Ginger wondered if he was waiting for applause. She knew he wouldn't get it because everyone was still in shock about poor Mr Wong.

'I know we're all still in shock about poor Mr Wong,' said Mr Napier, face suddenly grave. 'Mr and Mrs Smith are visiting him now, and we all hope he'll be back with us soon. In the meantime I'll be doing everything I can to keep the school running smoothly and happily. Starting with the dog problem.'

Ginger felt a tiny trickle of relief. At least he wasn't announcing her transfer. Instead he was grinning again.

'I did say dog problem,' said Mr Napier. 'Not bog problem.'

A few of Locklan Grosby's mates tittered.

'Bog problem?' whispered Isabel into Ginger's ear.

Ginger didn't know what Mr Napier was on about either.

'Fear not,' said Mr Napier. 'I will be dealing with our bog problem too. It's high time the fine teachers at this school had a hot tap in their toilets.'

He grinned around the hall like a smartypants kid.

Ginger saw that most of the teachers were grinning back.

She felt even sicker.

'But first,' said Mr Napier, suddenly serious again, 'we have an even more urgent problem to deal with. As most of you already know, last night poor Mr Wong was bitten by a savage dog.'

A few kids gasped.

Ginger wondered miserably if anyone would gasp like that when her transfer was announced.

'Yesterday,' continued Mr Napier, 'the same savage stray dog chased one of our students on her way to school and almost attacked her.'

'That's you,' hissed Isabel.

Ginger didn't reply. She was too busy thinking about what Mr Napier had just said.

How did he know it was the same dog? Mr Wong was bitten in the dark, so nobody could be sure it was even a dog at all. It could have just been a bad-tempered possum.

Ginger wondered if she should point this out to Mr Napier. She decided not to. Yelling out in assembly was a serious offence, specially for people who were in big trouble already.

Ginger felt Isabel nudge her.

She realised most of the people in the hall were looking at her. She felt her face go hot.

'Wave,' whispered Isabel. 'So they can see you're OK.'

It was a good thought, but Ginger didn't wave because she wasn't OK. Her guts were in a furball knot.

'I know I speak for everyone here,' continued Mr Napier, 'when I say that these dog attacks must stop. Our school must be protected. And I will take steps to make sure this happens.'

Ginger glanced around the hall. Nobody was smiling now. All eyes were on Mr Napier. Even Locklan Grosby and his mates were transfixed.

'I have already spoken to the council rangers,' said Mr Napier. 'Security will be stepped up. From today, no dangerous animal will be allowed in or near this school. We don't want any more unfortunate victims. Three are enough.'

Ginger frowned.

Three?

'That's right, three,' said Mr Napier, looking around the hall. 'Mr Wong. Ginger Smith. And Pets Day, which has been cancelled.'

There was a stunned silence.

Ginger struggled to make sense of this, and saw that everyone else was too.

Pets Day, cancelled?

A low moan rose from the kids. Whole classes were almost in tears. Teachers, looking pretty stunned themselves, were telling kids to be quiet.

Isabel looked like she was in pain. Locklan Grosby looked like someone had stolen his dad's Mercedes. Even Ned Timms looked upset, and he didn't even have a pet.

'I know I speak for everybody here,' said Mr Napier, 'when I say how much we all regret this sad but necessary decision.'

Ginger stared at Mr Napier.

He didn't look like he regretted it one bit.

He's just using the dog problem as an excuse, she thought. He's cancelled Pets Day because Cornflake messed up his hair and gave him a few scratches.

She felt a stab of indignation.

Tiny scratches that had healed already.

Suddenly Ginger felt sicker than she had all morning.

It was partly her fault.

If I hadn't made so much fuss about that dog yesterday morning, she thought, Mr Napier wouldn't have such a good excuse now.

Before Ginger could stop herself, she was on her feet, hand in the air.

'Mr Napier,' she called out. 'Permission to speak, please.'

Now even more people were staring at her. But nobody was telling her to sit down. Out of the corner of her eye Ginger could see Ms Shapcott, mouth gaping. Sometimes it was useful having a class teacher who went into shock easily.

Ginger carried on before Mr Napier could say no.

'It's not fair,' she said, surprised at how loud her voice sounded in the big hall. 'Nobody's going to be attacked on Pets Day. Pets aren't dangerous animals.'

She hoped Mr Napier had never seen Ricebubble when she was in a really sarcastic mood.

'Good on you,' whispered Isabel.

Mr Napier, not smiling now, looked down at Ginger for a long moment.

Ginger waited for streams of radioactive cat spray to squirt out of his eyes and melt her brain. Or for him to announce her transfer to another school.

Instead he just nodded slowly.

'Good point, Ginger,' he said. 'I'm glad you raised it. I didn't understand myself at first why Pets Day had to be cancelled. But then the student health people at the Education Department explained it to me. Animals don't have to attack to be dangerous, you see. Animals are dangerous to some people's health just by being in the school.'

Ginger didn't understand. She could see nobody else did either.

'The unfortunate people I'm talking about,' said Mr Napier, and Ginger saw he was looking straight at her, 'are the people who are allergic to animals.'

Ginger stared back at him, taking this in.

But, thought Ginger, going numb with horror, there's only one person in the school with an animal allergy.

Me.

Suddenly Ginger could only look at the floor. She wished it would turn into a huge cat's bum and swallow her up. Even Isabel's sympathetic hand on her arm didn't make her feel any better.

Everyone's favourite day in the whole school year had just been ruined, and everyone knew it was Ginger Smith's fault.

6

BARKING MAD

Ginger knocked on Mr Wong's office door, wishing she was somewhere else.

Trapped inside a dead tuna on a cat farm.

Anywhere but here.

She took a deep breath. This was where she had to be. She owed it to four hundred kids and teachers.

'Come in,' said Mr Napier's voice.

Ginger went in.

Mr Napier was sitting behind Mr Wong's desk. He didn't look like he wished he was somewhere else. He looked like he was very pleased to be exactly where he was.

'Ah, Miss Smith,' he said with a thin smile. 'I was expecting a visit from you.'

Ginger went over to the desk and tried to speak. Her mouth felt very dry, mostly from anxiety but partly from Mr Napier's aftershave fumes.

Whatever you do, Ginger told herself, don't sneeze.

She looked straight at Mr Napier.

'Please don't cancel Pets Day because of me,' she said. 'I'll stay away that day. I'll stay away all next week if you like.'

Ginger held her breath.

Please, she begged silently. Please agree.

Mr Napier didn't say anything, just fiddled with Mr Wong's pen.

Ginger felt cold despair uncurl inside her. He wasn't going to agree. She'd have to say it. It was all she had left.

'Transfer me to another school before next Thursday,' she said quietly. 'Then you won't have to cancel Pets Day.'

Mr Napier looked at her for a long time.

Ginger knew that whatever he said, yes or no, she'd have to struggle not to cry.

Mr Napier leaned back and put his feet up on Mr Wong's desk.

Ginger couldn't believe it.

A kid would get detention for that, even on a regular school desk. Mr Wong's desk was an antique. Mr Wong reckoned it was nearly thirty years old.

'Pets Day is cancelled,' said Mr Napier. 'But I do have some good news for you. I've decided to give you a second chance. You can stay at this school. For now.'

Ginger blinked hard.

It didn't feel like good news. Staying here with all the people she cared about. Seeing their disappointment every time they looked at her.

'But only if you stop being rude and disruptive,' said Mr Napier. 'And thinking you can get away with it just because your parents are teachers here.'

Ginger opened her mouth to tell him what a load of kitty litter that was, then closed it. He'd only think she was being rude and disruptive.

She glared at the floor.

Easy to see your parents were never teachers, she thought bitterly. Easy to see you've never been given a detention by your own mum and dad. Easy to see you've never had to get a nosebleed just to see them.

'What you don't understand,' said Mr Napier, 'is that I care about you.'

Ginger stared at him.

Cats care about mice, she thought, but not in a nice way.

'I care about your welfare,' continued Mr Napier. 'That's why I told the Education Department about your allergy.'

Mr Napier gave her another smile. It was a cat smile. Mouth, but no eyes.

'See,' he said. 'I care.'

Ginger's brain felt like Cornflake in a very small schoolbag.

He was playing with her. Torturing her. Just like Ricebubble did with grasshoppers and fishfingers.

Ginger didn't want to see that smile any more, so she looked away.

And almost gasped.

The walls of Mr Wong's office were bare. All Mr Wong's photos, the ones of his travels and his family and his old pets and his old students, were gone.

So were his Chinese art posters.

And his ice-skating certificates.

Ginger stared. Then she remembered Mr Napier was watching her.

'Where are Mr Wong's wall things?' she asked, trying not to sound rude or disruptive. Mr Napier might not realise how important family photos could be to people. There wasn't a single family photo of his anywhere on the desk or walls.

Ginger tried to look polite, but firm and accusing at the same time.

Mr Napier had the same expression on his face that Locklan Grosby got when he lied about how many times his dog had seen *Star Wars*.

For a second Ginger thought Mr Napier was going to lie too. Was going to tell her that Mr Wong hadn't been bitten by a dog, he'd been kidnapped by a private school. One that was desperate for a really good principal with really interesting things to hang in his office.

He didn't.

'I've put Mr Wong's things away safely,' said Mr Napier. 'Until I get a moment to send them to him.'

Something exploded in Ginger's head.

'You shouldn't have touched them,' she shouted. 'Some of those things are precious antique state championship ice-skating certificates and Mr Wong cares about them a lot and he'll be back in a couple of days and now he'll have to hang them all up again thanks to you.'

Ginger found she was panting, partly from shouting, and partly because Mr Napier was standing up, furious.

She took a step back.

She tried to remember if principals were allowed to cane kids these days. Mr Wong never did, but it might still be legal.

Suddenly the exotic smell of Ms Cunningham's perfume burst through the chemical haze of Mr Napier's aftershave.

Ms Cunningham stuck her head into the room.

Ginger saw the concerned look on her face. She seemed relieved that Ginger was OK.

'Excuse me,' said Ms Cunningham, flashing a smile at Mr Napier. 'I'm looking for a library volunteer. I thought I heard one in here. Have you finished with her?'

Mr Napier looked hard at Ginger for a moment.

'No,' he said, managing a smile. 'But I can wait.'

The library clock said nearly five-thirty when Ginger finished helping Ms Cunningham.

'Thank you so much, Ginger,' said Ms Cunningham, looking up from her computer. 'You're a trooper.'

Ginger's arms ached. It had been a huge job, shifting all the books to make room for a bigger section on Mexico. But she didn't mind. She was glad to give Ms Cunningham the chance to finish an urgent email to her Mexican boyfriend.

And it had been a good day.

As soon as she'd got to the library, Ms Cunningham had told her not to feel so bad about Pets Day because there were two kids in Year Two who were allergic to goldfish.

Ginger felt very moved by that.

Plus Ms Cunningham knew some really good jokes about library cataloguing data. And she taught Ginger how to pronounce the names of several Mexican holiday resorts. And when Ginger thanked Ms Cunningham for rescuing her, Ms Cunningham gave her some really good advice about Mr Napier.

'Stay away from him.'

Ginger planned to follow that advice if she could.

'I'm off now,' she said.

Ms Cunningham looked concerned. 'Are you sure you don't want a lift?'

'No thanks,' said Ginger. 'I'll be fine. I'd rather walk.'

Her legs ached, and her back, and a lift home would have been great, but there was something she had to do on the way.

Something that had to be secret for now, in case Mr Napier found out, or the Education Department.

She had to see Mr Wong to try and save Pets Day.

Ginger hurried across the playground.

She was pretty sure she could remember where Mr Wong lived because she'd been there with Mum and Dad. And if she didn't stay too long, she'd still be home at around the time Mum and Dad were expecting her.

Ginger headed for the school gate.

Then the smell hit her.

She froze.

Calm down, she told herself. It could be any dog. A friendly safe dog on a lead with its owner.

She sniffed the air.

Her throat went tight.

She knew that smell.

It was the dog from yesterday morning. The hungry one that had chased her. The one they reckoned had attacked Mr Wong.

Ginger looked around frantically, squinting for a sight of it, trying to work out which way to run.

She couldn't see the dog, but her nose told her it wasn't far away. The smell was coming from the netball court.

If I sprint, thought Ginger, I can be out the gate and on my way to Mr Wong's before it sees me.

Then she heard a voice coming from the netball court.

It was Mr Napier's voice.

She couldn't hear what he was saying and she couldn't see him because most of the netball court was behind the tuckshop. But it was definitely him.

He was just talking normally, not shouting or pleading or screaming or anything. He didn't sound like a man who had any idea a savage dog was close.

Ginger started running towards the gate.

She stopped.

I can't do it, she thought. Ms Cunningham's advice was really good and I know I should be keeping as far away from Mr Napier as I can, but I can't leave a human being on a netball court not realising he's being stalked by a vicious brute.

I've got to go and warn him.

7

HAVING KITTENS

Ginger crept towards the netball court.

She sniffed the air.

The savage dog smell was stronger than ever.

Ginger could still hear Mr Napier's voice coming from behind the tuckshop. She couldn't make out exactly what he was saying, but he didn't sound like a man who had a clue how much danger he was in.

Ginger peeked round the corner of the tuckshop.

And gasped.

Mr Napier was talking to Bruno the handyman. One of Bruno's legs was bandaged from halfway up his shin to just below his shorts. Ginger couldn't see any blood, but with a bandage that size the wound must be huge.

Mr Napier was looking at his watch.

'Where are they?' he said. 'I rang them forty minutes ago.'

That'll be the ambulance, thought Ginger. Poor Bruno. Why doesn't Mr Napier let him lie down?

He's got a dog bite the size of a fuguggling cat flap.

She looked around anxiously, wondering where the blood-crazed dog was.

Bruno and Mr Napier didn't seem worried.

They must be in shock.

'Is that them?' said Bruno, pointing.

Ginger saw two people hurrying over from the side gate. They didn't look like ambulance officers. One was a woman in a dark suit carrying a note-book, the other was a bloke in jeans with a camera bag. They looked to Ginger like a journalist and a photographer.

'Sorry,' said the journalist to Mr Napier. 'Never try to do a quick interview with a pensioner who can play tunes on toilet paper.' She pointed. 'Is that it?'

Ginger gasped again.

The journalist was pointing to the wire cage where the netballs were kept.

Shut in the cage, half-hidden by balls, was a black shape.

'That's the savage brute,' said Mr Napier.

Because Ginger didn't dare stick her head right round the corner of the tuckshop she couldn't see perfectly, but her nose told her it was the dog from yesterday morning. It seemed to be lying with its head on its paws, tail drooping. Ginger could hear it panting. Bruno must have given it a major blast with the leaf-blower.

The journalist saw Bruno's bandage and her eyes went wide.

'Did the dog do that?' she said.

Bruno shook his head. 'I fell off a cliff last night,' he said. 'Indoor rock-climbing.'

Of course, thought Ginger. Bruno was into extreme sports. He was always falling off snowboards and crashing hang-gliders.

Mr Napier cleared his throat.

'It was our previous principal who was attacked and savaged by this vicious beast,' he said.

Ginger shuddered. Savaged? She hoped for poor Mr Wong's sake that Mr Napier was exaggerating.

'But,' continued Mr Napier, 'it could easily have been Bruno here as well. Or one of several hundred innocent kiddies. That's why, for the safety of the entire school community, I am taking firm and decisive action to …'

'So it was actually you who caught the animal, was it?' said the journalist.

Mr Napier glared at her for interrupting.

'No,' said Bruno proudly. 'It was me.'

Mr Napier glared at Bruno.

'I'm trying to do an interview,' he said. 'Shouldn't you be dog-proofing our external fences as we discussed earlier?'

'OK,' said Bruno. He threw a wistful glance at the photographer's camera, then limped away.

For a fearful second, Ginger thought he was coming in her direction, but he didn't.

'As I was saying,' continued Mr Napier to the journalist, 'on behalf of the entire school I am taking firm and decisive action to protect this community from …'

'Actually,' said the journalist, 'can we do the photo first? The photographer's got to do a gardening club camellia-swap in ten minutes.'

By the time the photographer finished snapping Mr Napier in front of the cage, and Mr Napier suggested to the journalist that they do the interview in his office over a cup of tea, and they went inside, Ginger's back was killing her.

She'd been crouched next to the tuckshop, straining her ears, for what felt like hours. The straps of her schoolbag were nearly ripping her shoulders off.

Ginger stood up and groaned.

She was parched.

I bet the dog is too, she thought.

She could hear it panting more loudly now. Its shaggy coat was going up and down. So was Ginger's chest at the thought of going close.

Ginger stared over at the cage, torn.

She knew she should be heading for Mr Wong's place as fast as she could. As well as begging him to help save Pets Day, she wanted to make sure he wasn't badly hurt. But she couldn't leave the dog without a drink. Even violent criminals in jail got drinks.

Ginger hurried over to the bubbler. She pulled her school hat out of her bag, filled it with water and hurried over to the cage.

As she got closer she slowed down.

The dog was staring at her.

She stepped nearer, watching the dog just as closely as it was watching her.

She couldn't see any vicious signs. Its teeth were big, but it couldn't help that, just like Ms Shapcott couldn't help having a big nose. There was something scary about the way its big shoulders were hunched, but that was probably just stress from the leaf-blower. Its eyes were sad and gentle.

Ginger checked herself for cat hairs. No point inflaming the dog and making this more dangerous than it already was.

She gritted her teeth and bent down and squeezed her hat through the wire of the cage. She wanted to pull her hands away immediately, but realised if she did the sides of the hat would flop down and the water would leak out.

The dog stared up at her.

Ginger remembered she'd just been pressing herself against the tuckshop wall for a long time. The dog probably hadn't seen brick marks on a human face before.

'They'll fade,' said Ginger. 'Come on, drink.'

The dog drank, lapping noisily.

Then, before Ginger could pull away, the dog licked her hand.

Fuguggle.

Ginger snatched her hand away and slumped back, weak with shock.

That dog was quick. It could have had her whole hand off. She could be sitting there bleeding onto the netball court from a stump.

But it hadn't, and she wasn't.

Its tongue had been rough, and cold from the water. Instead of a stump, Ginger had a warm tingle on the back of her hand.

The dog was looking at her, water dripping off its whiskers, a patient expression on its face. It was the expression Isabel got when Locklan Grosby laughed at her for saying goldfish were more intelligent than people.

Ginger felt a pang of regret for pulling her hand away and hurting the dog's feelings.

'Sorry,' she said.

Slowly, pretty sure that doing this meant that goldfish were more intelligent than her, Ginger slid her hand back through the wire.

The dog licked it again.

This time she left it there.

The dog kept licking until suddenly a shadow fell over them.

Ginger spun round.

'Sorry to startle you,' said the photographer. He bent down and picked up a small leather pouch from the ground. 'Forgot my light meter.'

Ginger couldn't speak. The panic of thinking it was Mr Napier had frozen her throat.

'Rrrgghh,' she said.

'Rrrgghh,' growled the dog in reply.

The photographer looked surprised. Then he frowned down at the dog.

'Poor blighter,' he said. 'You've had it now, haven't you, boy?' He looked at Ginger. 'And you want to be careful, sticking your hand in there. See you.'

He turned away towards the side gate.

'Wait,' said Ginger. 'What's going to happen to him?'

The photographer stopped and turned back to her.

Ginger could see he had the look on his face that adults get when they know something but don't think they should tell a kid. The look Mum and Dad got when Ginger asked them why she was the only one in the family with freckles.

'Not good,' said the photographer. 'He'll be taken to the pound and if they can't find his owner, which they won't, they'll give him two weeks. If nobody wants to adopt him in two weeks, which they won't …'

The photographer shrugged.

'Why won't somebody want to adopt him?' said Ginger.

'Look at the size of him,' said the photographer. 'The pound's full of big monsters like him. People want cute and little. The stupid idiots get puppies, go into shock when they grow big, and dump them.'

'So what'll happen to him?' said Ginger.

The photographer got that look on his face again.

Come on, thought Ginger. I'm tough. I know about the world.

The photographer ran a finger across his throat.

Ginger felt faint.

'Sorry,' said the photographer. 'But it's the truth. You mind your hands, OK?'

Ginger waited while the photographer drove off. By the time the car engine had faded away, she knew what she had to do.

'Look,' she said to the dog. 'I don't know if you attacked Mr Wong or not. But I do know that people who kill whole football teams and things still get a fair trial in court. They don't get dumped in a pound and two weeks later get their throat cut.'

The dog looked even sadder than before.

Ginger realised she probably shouldn't have mentioned the throat bit.

'Sorry,' she said. 'And don't be startled by what I'm going to do now.'

She stood up and gave the padlock on the cage some really hard kicks.

The padlock had been broken for years. The teachers had agreed not to get a new one so they wouldn't have to worry about who had the key.

On the fifth kick the padlock fell off.

Ginger gripped the wire lid of the cage.

OK, she thought. Here goes.

She threw open the lid and took several quick steps backwards.

The dog didn't hesitate. He leaped out of the cage and flung himself at Ginger.

She tried to scream, but before she could, she realised the dog was licking her knee.

'Go,' she croaked.

The dog looked up at her, head on one side.

'Run,' she said. 'Get out of here.'

The dog took a few steps back, eyes narrowing.

'Please,' yelled Ginger.

She hurled her soggy hat at the dog.

The dog gave her a long look, then turned and ran across the netball court and out the side gate.

When he'd disappeared down the street, Ginger started breathing again.

Justice, she said to herself. Even dogs deserve justice. Which is more than I'll get if Mr Napier finds out what I've done.

8

MARROWBONE JELLY

'Ginger,' said Mrs Wong, beaming. 'How tjorkmin lovely to see you. Come in.'

Ginger smiled back and followed her into the house, wondering what exactly Mrs Wong had said. Her Norwegian accent could be a bit strong at times.

'Do you like my new swearword?' asked Mrs Wong. 'Mr Wong told me about your father's Year Six project and I thought I'd have a go.'

'It's very good,' said Ginger. 'How's Mr Wong?'

Mrs Wong sighed. 'Not so tjorkmin bad, considering,' she said. 'He's had a nasty shock of course, but once he gets the stitches out I think he'll start to mend.'

Mr Wong's voice floated down the hall.

'Is that Ginger Smith I hear?'

Ginger was shocked.

Mr Wong sounded weak and sort of mumbly, as if his throat was all swollen.

'He's in here,' said Mrs Wong, opening the living room door.

Ginger stepped in, dreading what she'd see. What if Mr Napier was right? What if poor Mr Wong had been savaged? What if he was so badly chewed he'd be in pain for the rest of his life and never be able to come back to school?

'G'day Ginger,' said Mr Wong, waving a half-eaten sandwich at her with a smile.

Ginger blinked with relief. She could see now why Mr Wong's voice sounded funny. He was stuffing his face.

She went over to where he was sitting on an armchair with his foot up on a pile of books. He didn't look very chewed at all. In fact, apart from his bandaged foot, there wasn't a single toothmark on him, assuming he was OK under his pyjama shorts.

'How are you, Mr Wong?' said Ginger.

Mr Wong swallowed and his wrinkles drooped into sadness.

'Terrible,' he said. 'I've been dropped from the state under-25 ice-skating team.' He winked at Ginger. 'But apart from that I'm not so bad.'

'Tjorkmin old fool,' said Mrs Wong.

'These are for you,' said Ginger, handing Mr Wong the flowers she'd brought for him. 'They're from the whole school.'

She thought it was only fair to say that, seeing as they'd come from the flower bed outside the staff room.

'They're lovely,' said Mr Wong. 'My favourites. That's why I got Bruno to plant them. Would you like a sweet-and-sour pork sandwich?'

He held out his plate to Ginger.

'Thanks,' she said, taking one and avoiding his eyes.

'Sit down,' said Mrs Wong. 'I'll get you a cold drink.'

Mr Wong waited till his wife was out of the room, then gave Ginger a mischievous look.

'I met Mrs Wong on a frozen lake in Norway,' he said. 'When I was an exchange student. She tried to do a spin on her skates and sprained her ankle. I had to nurse her for six days.' He chuckled. 'Now it's my turn. I've been waiting forty-seven years for this.'

Ginger smiled.

She was relieved to see that the bandage on Mr Wong's foot was only about a quarter the size of Bruno's.

Probably just a nibble, she thought as she chewed her sandwich.

Which meant Mr Wong wouldn't mind her asking for his help to save Pets Day.

'Mr Wong,' she said. 'Pets Day's been cancelled.'

Mr Wong sighed and nodded, and suddenly he looked very old and weary.

'I know,' he said. 'Your mum and dad visited me this morning.'

'Isn't there anything you can do?' blurted Ginger. 'Like get Mr Napier booted out?'

Mr Wong frowned.

'Sorry,' said Ginger. 'I didn't mean to be rude, but …'

'That's OK,' said Mr Wong. 'I understand how you feel. But I'm afraid while I'm away, Mr Napier's the boss. And if the Education Department have said no Pets Day, there's nothing any of us can do.'

Ginger thought frantically.

'Can't you tell them what clean pets we have at our school?' she said. 'If you like I can take Isabel's goldfish to their office and let it swim around in their water cooler for a day to prove it.'

Mr Wong smiled sadly.

'I'm sorry Ginger,' he said. 'I'm as upset about this as you are.'

Suddenly Mr Wong looked very upset. He scrunched up his face and closed his eyes. Ginger realised he was in pain.

'Mrs Wong,' she yelled.

Mrs Wong hurried in and took Mr Wong's hand.

'I think it's bleeding again,' he said.

'I'll adjust the dressing,' she said.

'Shall I go?' asked Ginger.

'No,' said Mrs Wong. 'You haven't had your drink yet. Just don't look.'

But Ginger did look. She couldn't stop herself. When she saw what was under Mr Wong's bandage, she wished she'd listened to Mrs Wong.

'That must hurt heaps,' she said in a small voice after Mrs Wong had finished.

Mr Wong shrugged, but Ginger knew it was just a brave principal way of saying yes.

She'd planned to tell Mr Wong about Mr Napier threatening to get her transferred, but he looked so pale and weak now she didn't want to make things worse.

Plus there was something else she needed to ask him.

'Mr Wong,' she said. 'Did you see the dog that bit you?'

'No,' said Mr Wong. 'It was too dark. Thanks for reminding me. I must get Bruno to fix that light in the teachers' carpark.'

Scary thoughts filled Ginger's head. For a second she was tempted to confess to Mr Wong what she'd done less than an hour ago.

She decided not to.

The questions bouncing around in her head were too awful.

What if she'd been wrong?

What if the dog she'd set free was the one that had done what she'd just seen under poor Mr Wong's bandage?

Then, thought Ginger miserably, a savage monster is roaming the streets, and it's my fault.

9

LYING DOGGO

'Would you like a lift home?' asked Mrs Wong at the front gate.

Yes, said Ginger silently, I would. I'd like a lift very much, thank you. And a leaf-blower.

'No thanks,' said Ginger out loud. 'I'll be fine. My place is only ten minutes away.'

Mrs Wong looked doubtful.

Ginger had a stern word with herself.

You can't drag an old lady out in her car when it's getting dark. Not just because you're having wild and silly thoughts about dogs and working yourself up into a state.

'I'll be OK,' said Ginger to Mrs Wong. 'I walk home by myself all the time.'

Mrs Wong looked a bit less worried.

'Anyway,' said Ginger. 'They've probably caught that dog by now.'

'I tjorkmin hope so,' said Mrs Wong.

They both smiled.

Ginger suddenly felt almost certain she wouldn't be seeing the dog again.

Ginger was halfway home when she saw the dog.

It was following her.

'Oh, fuguggle,' she said under her breath.

She walked faster and spent the next couple of minutes trying to convince herself it was a cat. A big dark cat that was only following her because it had heard there was a laundry basket at her place that was really good for shedding hair in.

Ginger peeked over her shoulder.

It wasn't a cat.

Even at that distance in the dusk she could see the dog's dark shiny fur and the muscly shape of its shoulders. She could also see that, apart from her and the dog, the street was deserted.

Ginger walked as fast as she could without actually running.

Think friendly, she said to herself. Think friendly.

She remembered how the dog had licked her hand.

And her knee.

And looked at her with sad eyes.

Then she remembered how Ricebubble could be the friendliest cat in the world. Just for a couple of minutes. Just to suck you in. And then, while you were sneezing, she'd knock the hairdryer into the sink and try to electrocute you.

Maybe, thought Ginger, panic rising, that's what

happened to poor Mr Wong. Maybe the dog licked his hand in such a friendly way that Mr Wong lifted his trouser leg so the dog could lick his knee, but it was all a plot and instead the dog tried to gnaw through his ankle.

Ginger ran.

Her schoolbag was too heavy.

The Chinese medicine books Mr Wong had lent her because they had stuff in them about cat allergies were weighing her down and giving her a stitch.

The dog was getting closer.

Without slowing down Ginger stuck her arms out behind her and leaned back and let the bag slide off. She heard it thud onto the footpath.

That was better.

Now she could run.

Only two streets to go.

Except the stitch was still there.

Getting worse.

In about ten seconds, thought Ginger, gritting her teeth with the pain, I'll have to stop.

She looked around wildly for a front door to bash on. She could smell dinners cooking and car engines cooling. Trouble was, which door? Some people went out to movies and left crockpots simmering and their second car in the driveway to fool burglars.

If I pick the wrong door, thought Ginger, that brute'll have its teeth in my ankle before I can get over the fence to the next house.

Suddenly, as she staggered round the corner into Nauru Crescent, she smelled something else.

Something sweet and musty and rotten and revolting.

'Thank you,' she croaked under her breath. 'Thank you.'

Ginger hauled herself up into the tangled branches and tumbling blossoms of Mr O'Shaunessy's Bolivian fig tree and crouched panting there, trying not to throw up. She said a silent prayer of thanks to Mr O'Shaunessy for planting such a foul-smelling thing in his front yard.

OK, not everyone thought it was foul-smelling. Just those with a keen sense of smell. Her and dogs, mostly.

Ginger forced herself to stop panting.

This was the one place for miles around where the dog wouldn't be able to smell her. If she kept quiet and didn't move, the darkness would hide her.

She hoped.

In the distance she could hear the dog panting. It was a fair way off but getting closer. There was another sound too. One she didn't recognise. A sound like toast being scraped.

That's strange, thought Ginger. I can't smell any toast.

The sound got closer.

So did the dog's panting.

Suddenly Ginger knew what the sound was. Something heavy being dragged along the footpath.

Oh no, she thought. The dog's attacked someone else and now it's dragging their mutilated body to somewhere the police won't find it.

Ginger leaned forward on the branch, trying to catch a glimpse of the horrible crime in case she ever had to give evidence in court or at the pound.

Her nose brushed a fig flower.

Fuguggle, she thought.

Pollen.

The sneeze was so huge it flung her out of the tree. Mr O'Shaunessy's front lawn rushed up out of the gloom and whacked her in the chest.

Ginger lay there for a long time, dazed and groaning.

This must be my punishment, she thought. For causing Pets Day to be cancelled and letting a vicious brute go free.

Slowly her sneeze tears dried and her chest stopped hurting and she realised she wasn't injured.

She forced herself to think about the dog.

It may not be able to smell me here, she thought, but it sure as fuguggle would have heard my groans.

Ginger kept her eyes closed. Perhaps if the dog thought she was dead it would leave her alone. Specially as it already had a corpse.

No such luck.

Something rough and warm brushed against her

hand. The dog was so close she could smell it even over the fig-tree pong.

Ginger opened her eyes.

The dog's big body loomed over her. In the street lights its fur was a frizzy halo. It started licking her hand and watching her intently.

Ginger went rigid. Was this a plot? A cunning plan to discover if she was alive so it could kill her?

Its eyes looked too gentle for that.

Then Ginger saw something else. There, next to the dog, on the grass.

Her schoolbag.

Ginger stared at it.

She stared at the dog.

Amazing. That must have been the sound. The dog dragging her bag along the street to give it back to her.

'Thanks,' she whispered.

Except her throat was still rigid with shock and amazement and it came out more like 'rrrgghh.'

'Rrrgghh,' replied the dog softly.

Suddenly Ginger wanted to pat him.

Before she could, headlights splayed down the street. A vehicle was slowly cruising towards them. Ginger peered into the glare, trying to see if it was Dad out looking for her.

It wasn't. The vehicle had a sign on its roof with one word lit up.

Ranger.

Ginger tensed again.

Dog patrol.

The rangers must be doing extra patrols because of Mr Napier's nagging.

Ginger grabbed the dog and her bag and tried to drag them both behind the trunk of the Bolivian fig tree. Dragging a dog that size was even harder than dragging an adult. Ginger didn't get very far until the dog realised what she was trying to do and took her schoolbag in his teeth and carried it behind the tree for her.

She crouched next to the dog and stroked his back to say thank you, and stroked his nose so he'd smell her instead of the fig-tree pong.

Don't stop, she silently begged the ranger vehicle.

It didn't.

Ginger stayed close to the dog until the vehicle had turned into the next street and the sound of its engine had died away into the night.

The dog was trembling.

I'm not surprised, thought Ginger.

'Don't worry,' she whispered into his big furry ear. 'That stuff I said before about throats being cut. I'm not going to let that happen to you. I'm going to find somewhere safe for you to hide.'

10

IN THE DOG HOUSE

Ginger dumped her schoolbag behind the settee so nobody would notice the teeth marks on the strap. Then she went into the kitchen, trying not to look like someone who'd just hidden a dog in the back shed.

'There you are, pet.'

Mum was stirring a saucepan with one hand and holding the phone to her ear with the other.

'Where have you been?' she asked Ginger. 'No, not you, Mrs Funicello. Yes, I am listening. You're telling me how disappointed Lucrezia and the goat are about Pets Day being cancelled.'

Dad looked up at Ginger from the kitchen bench where he was chopping vegetables and marking an exercise book.

'We were getting worried,' he said. 'Ms Cunningham told us you'd be home half an hour ago. I was going to call the police once Mum was off the phone.'

Ginger was pretty sure he was joking, but decided to tell the truth anyway.

Well, some of it.

'I went to visit Mr Wong,' she said. 'To see how he is.'

Dad sighed. 'Poor bloke,' he said. 'When I saw his ankle, it made me glad we've got cats and not dogs.'

Ginger didn't reply. Instead she kept an ear cocked towards the backyard.

It'll be OK, she thought, as long as the dog doesn't bark.

'Dad,' said Mitzi, pointing. 'What's wrong with Cornflake and Ricebubble?'

Ginger looked up.

The two cats were on top of the fridge, glaring and hissing. Madonna was in a state too, backing into the bread bin and scowling. Cher and Kylie were both trying to squeeze into the cupboard under the sink.

Ginger realised all the cats were glaring at her with fury and outrage.

Fuguggle, she thought. They can smell the dog on me.

'That's weird,' said Dad. 'Wonder what's upsetting them?'

'Must be me,' said Ginger. 'I'm not very popular with anyone at the moment.'

Ginger opened the shed door as quietly as she could.

The dog didn't bark.

'Good boy,' whispered Ginger, relieved.

She wasn't sure if the dog was keeping quiet because he was very smart and knew how sensitive teachers were to noise when they were in their bedroom marking assignments, or if he was just weak with hunger.

Ginger put the plate down in front of the dog.

She shone the torch on it.

'It's chicken schnitzel,' she said. 'Sorry. The only meat in the freezer was a leg of lamb and it would have taken too long to defrost in the microwave.'

She realised the dog wasn't listening.

He was gobbling the food, shoulders hunched, ears flat to his head.

Ginger was pleased to see he was eating the peas and cauliflower too. She'd seen on TV once how orphans and abandoned family members who had to live on the streets often didn't get enough vegetables.

'The reason there's pasta sauce on the vegies,' she whispered, 'is that I don't like them without it and I thought you might feel the same way.'

The dog looked up at her, pasta sauce and peas glistening on his jaws. Ginger could see in his eyes that he did feel the same way and that he was very grateful.

Then he barked.

Just once.

It was so loud Ginger almost dropped the torch.

'Sshhh,' she hissed frantically. 'Mum and Dad'll hear you.'

'Too late,' said Dad's voice.

Ginger spun round.

Mum and Dad were standing at the shed door, looking at her and the dog with grim expressions.

Ginger felt numb with shock. She forced herself to speak.

'He's not savage,' she said. 'He's friendly.' She gestured around the shed. 'See, he hasn't attacked any of the garden tools, or the potting mix.'

Mum and Dad didn't seem impressed.

'Whose animal is this?' demanded Mum.

'Nobody's,' said Ginger. 'Mine.'

Mum peered warily at the dog. 'Is that the one that chased you on the way to school yesterday?' she said.

'He didn't chase me,' said Ginger. 'He just wanted to make friends. He must have known we're a family of animal lovers.'

Mum and Dad still didn't look impressed. Ginger decided she'd better change the subject.

'How did you know he was here?' she asked. 'I was very quiet so I wouldn't disturb you.'

'Oh,' said Mum. 'Little clues. The freezer door wide open. Chicken schnitzel in the sink. Pasta sauce splattered over the microwave.'

Ginger sighed with exasperation. That was the trouble with parents. How could they be so obsessed with tiny details when a dog's life was at stake?

Dad reached into the shed, grabbed Ginger and dragged her out.

74

'Royce Napier reckons this brute attacked Mr Wong,' said Dad. 'I'm calling the rangers.'

'No,' begged Ginger. 'He's innocent. Please don't call them. He'll be killed.'

The words came out before she could stop them. She looked back at the dog, hoping he wasn't feeling too upset by this news.

The dog didn't look upset. He was standing there watching them all and licking pasta sauce off his chin.

Dad slammed the shed door.

'That brute certainly doesn't look innocent,' said Dad. 'And I'm not taking the risk.'

'He carried my schoolbag for me,' said Ginger. 'Is that the act of a violent criminal?'

Mum and Dad looked at each other.

'It's too late to ring the rangers now,' said Mum. 'We'll keep it in the shed tonight and ring them in the morning.'

As they led her away, Ginger gave the dog a look through the shed window to let him know that all this wasn't so bad.

A whole night was plenty of time to change people's minds.

Even teachers.

Ginger peeked in through the back door.

All clear.

Mum and Dad must still be working upstairs.

'Remember,' Ginger whispered to the dog. 'The

cats aren't used to having a dog around, so if they behave rudely, please don't be offended and please please don't eat any of them.'

The dog looked up at her and she could tell from his understanding expression that it was going to be OK.

Gently she ushered the dog inside.

Mitzi looked up from the TV.

'What are you doing?' she shrieked.

'Shhh,' whispered Ginger. 'It's OK. We're all going to watch TV quietly together so when Mum and Dad come down they'll see he's not a savage brute, just a quiet and lovable member of the family.'

Mitzi scowled nervously at the dog, then at Ginger. 'We're still going to watch The Simpsons,' she said.

Ginger sighed. 'Normally it's polite to let guests choose,' she said, 'but I'm not going to make a big thing of it.'

She turned to the cats.

This was the tricky bit.

Madonna was rigid in her pot plant, gaping at the dog in shock. Cher was on the back of the settee, stiff with disbelief. Kylie, who'd been dozing on the coffee table, was looking like she'd just woken up into a nightmare.

'Everybody,' said Ginger, 'this is our new family member. You'll find he's very nice once you get used to the size of his teeth. Please make him welcome.'

None of the cats moved.

Ginger decided this was a good thing, given how bitchy cats could be with their body language.

Then Cornflake and Ricebubble came into the room.

They saw the dog and leaped onto the dresser, knocking over most of Mum's china cats. The sudden noise snapped the rest of the cats out of their daze.

Madonna tried to climb up the pot plant, dragging the whole thing crashing onto the floor.

Cher scrambled up the curtain.

'Don't,' said Ginger. 'It's only decorative.'

Too late. The curtain tore away from the rod and Cher slid down the window, claws screeching against the glass.

There was a dull explosion.

Ginger turned and saw smoke wafting up from the DVD player, which Kylie had knocked off the top of the TV in a frantic attempt to get onto the ceiling.

Ricebubble flung herself off the dresser onto Ginger's chest.

Ginger gave a massive sneeze. She felt Ricebubble leap off her onto Mitzi.

Mitzi started yelling.

The cats were all hissing.

The only calm one, Ginger saw through the sneeze tears, was the dog, standing there watching the mayhem with a puzzled expression.

Mum and Dad burst into the room.

'What,' yelled Dad, 'is going on?'

'It wasn't the dog's fault,' said Ginger. 'The cats just got over-excited.'

Mum and Dad saw the dog.

'Brian,' said Mum. 'Get that brute back into the shed.'

Dad snatched up the rug and advanced on the dog like a nervous bullfighter. The dog looked at him for a moment, then trotted over to the back door.

'Mum,' begged Ginger. 'Give him a chance. He's friendly, look. Can't we keep him?'

For a second Ginger thought Mum was going to explode.

'In case you hadn't noticed,' said Mum, 'your father and I are both teachers at a school whose principal has been savagely attacked by a stray dog. What do you imagine the parents of the school are going to think if we not only fail to hand over the chief suspect, but let him move into our house?'

'There's no proof he bit Mr Wong,' said Ginger.

Sometimes, when teachers got really worked up, legal arguments were the only thing left.

'There's no proof he didn't,' yelled Dad from outside. 'Unless you've got DNA evidence.'

Ginger slumped onto the settee in despair.

She always lost arguments when Dad got scientific.

11

FLEE COLLAR

Ginger carefully placed the shed door on the ground and led the dog across the dark backyard.

She wished she was as used to midnight escapes as the dog obviously was. Her chest was going like a leaf-blower. The dog wasn't even panting.

He probably had a restful sleep, thought Ginger. Not like me, lying awake stressed for three hours waiting for Mum and Dad to turn their light off.

No wonder teachers were always exhausted, if they all went to bed that late.

Ginger stopped dead.

In the moonlight she could see a pair of eyes glaring at her and the dog.

Sprung.

Her brain raced.

It wasn't Mum or Dad because the eyes were too close together and too low down as well.

An angry meow rang out across the backyard.

It was what she'd feared.

Ricebubble.

Ginger put her hand on the dog's back, hoping he'd get the message not to eat Ricebubble or do anything else too noisy.

Then she reached into her schoolbag and pulled out the box of cat food she'd brought along in case this happened.

'Please,' she whispered to Ricebubble. 'Just keep quiet, OK? I know he's a dog and you're a cat, but please try and overlook the difference just this once.'

Before Ricebubble had a chance to argue, Ginger poured a big pile of cat food onto the ground.

Ricebubble's eyes widened and Ginger felt panic rising. If Ricebubble decided to pick a fight or get stuck into her about Pets Day, most of the street would be woken up.

But Ricebubble just stepped forward and started eating. The crunching was fairly loud, but not too bad.

'Thanks,' whispered Ginger.

She turned to the dog.

'Come on,' she said. 'Let's find you a safer place to hide.'

Ginger tapped softly on Isabel's bedroom window.

No answer.

She peered in through the curtains. The room was completely dark.

'It's one o'clock in the morning,' Ginger whispered to the dog. 'She must be in there.'

The dog looked as though he agreed.

Ginger banged a bit more loudly.

'Isabel's always been a heavy sleeper,' Ginger explained to the dog. 'Specially in class.'

She hoped Isabel's mum and dad were heavy sleepers too.

The light in the room came on, and Isabel's crumpled face appeared at the window. When she saw Ginger, it went smooth with surprise.

'What do you want?' she croaked, sliding the window open. 'It's the middle of the shiddleponging night.'

For an awful second Ginger thought Isabel still hadn't forgiven her about Pets Day. Then she reminded herself that Isabel was her best friend.

'I need a hiding place,' said Ginger. 'For an innocent suspect.'

Isabel saw the dog and her expression froze.

'Don't worry,' said Ginger. 'He's not violent.'

She reached in and grabbed Isabel's hand and pulled it down close to the dog.

Isabel gave a squeak of terror.

'It's OK,' said Ginger to the dog. 'She washes her hands a lot.'

The dog licked Isabel's hand.

While he did, Ginger explained the injustice the dog was facing.

Isabel started to calm down, but Ginger could see she was still pretty tense.

'I wish I could help,' said Isabel. 'But you can't hide him here. This is a goldfish house.'

'What about your shed?' asked Ginger.

'Mum and Dad use it all the time,' said Isabel. 'The clothes and books and hairdryers their church collects for the poor people in Africa, they store them in there.'

Ginger felt desperation clawing at her.

If Isabel couldn't help, who could?

'I know,' said Isabel. 'Ned Timms hasn't got any animals at his place.'

Yes, thought Ginger. Brilliant.

You could always trust a best friend to come up with a great idea, even if she couldn't come up with a shed.

Ginger and Isabel tapped softly on Ned's bedroom window.

A face that wasn't Ned's peered out at them.

'Shiddlepong,' whispered Isabel.

For a moment Ginger thought they'd got the wrong room, or even the wrong house. Then she remembered Ned shared a room with two of his brothers.

The brother looked at them for a while, then muttered something over his shoulder.

Ginger was pretty sure he said, 'It's that kid who ruined Pets Day.'

The brother disappeared and Ned's anxious face squinted out at them. He fumbled the window open.

'Are you OK?' he said.

Ginger explained about the dog and the injustice and the need for a shed.

Ned's face fell. 'Sorry,' he said, 'Gavin and Callum and Sean sleep in ours.'

Ginger guessed they were brothers rather than pets.

Ned was looking wistfully out the window at the dog. Suddenly his face lit up.

'I know a shed,' he said excitedly. 'I saw it when I went to help Dad at work. It's never used these days because it's old and they've got a new one with a roller door.'

Ginger sighed. She was grateful for the offer, but the factory where Mr Timms worked was about ten suburbs away. It'd be morning before they got over there. If Mum and Dad woke up and found her gone, they'd call the police and the army and probably the SAS.

'Thanks,' she said, 'but your dad's factory's too far.'

'I'm not talking about the factory,' said Ned. 'Dad's got a second job at weekends. It's only about ten minutes away.'

Ginger wanted to hug Ned, but decided not to in case he panicked. She hugged the dog instead.

Ginger didn't recognise where they were, but it didn't matter because the shed was perfect.

It was hidden away under some trees a long way from the new shed. The door wasn't even padlocked, just held shut with a twist of wire. And there were no windows so nobody would be peeking in.

'It's great,' whispered Ginger to Ned. 'Thanks.'

The dog obviously felt the same way because he was the first inside.

Ginger followed him in and shone the torch around. The shed was bigger than the one at home and apart from a few dead flowers in the corner it was completely empty.

'He's got room to run around in here,' said Ned.

Ginger gave the torch to Isabel and unpacked her schoolbag. On the floor she spread Mum and Dad's picnic blanket. It had a couple of holes in it, but it was the only blanket she'd been able to find that wasn't covered in cat hairs.

Next to it she placed the leg of lamb.

'Sorry I can't cut this up,' she said to the dog. 'It's still frozen. Plus I didn't bring a knife.'

The dog didn't look as though he minded.

Ginger poured water from her drink bottle into a bowl.

'It's one of Mum's matching set,' she said, 'so try not to break it.'

The dog looked puzzled till Ginger explained that she was actually speaking to Ned, who was a bit clumsy with his feet.

Ned didn't argue. He patted the dog's head.

'What's his name?' he asked.

Ginger looked at the dog. She'd never thought about it. The dog must have had an owner once and he must have a name, but he didn't have a collar so she had no way of knowing.

'Fang,' said Isabel. 'Cause he's got big teeth.'

'If I had a dog,' said Ned, 'I'd call it Roly.'

Neither of those felt right to Ginger. The dog didn't look very enthusiastic either.

As she gazed at him, Ginger had a sudden memory of a dog she'd seen in a picture book when she was little. It had fascinated her, that proud strong picture-book dog. She'd stared at it for hours, and not just because it had three heads.

Its name was Cerberus.

'Cerberus,' said Ginger.

The dog's ears pricked up and he looked at her.

It could have just been a trick of the torchlight, but she was pretty sure he was smiling.

Ginger smiled back. It was good to see someone with a name they liked. You appreciated things like that when you were named after a dead cat.

'Cerberus,' said Isabel, trying it out.

'Cerberus,' said Ned, sounding as though he quite liked it.

The dog looked as though he liked it a lot.

'Cerberus,' said Ginger, to let them know she'd decided.

Then it was time to go.

'I'll be back tomorrow,' said Ginger, giving Cerberus a hug. 'You'll be safe here.'

Cerberus licked her hand and she knew that was his way of saying thanks.

As they crept back to the hole they'd dug under the fence, Ginger took a closer look at where they were.

Her torchlight slid across lawns and paths and clumps of flowers. Dotted all around were rocks and little slabs of concrete with writing on them.

Ginger bent down and read one.

'In Loving Memory,' it said. 'Binky. Not Gone, Just Sleeping In His Kennel In Heaven.'

A chill ran down Ginger's back under her schoolbag.

Suddenly she knew where they were.

'Ned,' she hissed. 'This is the pet cemetery. We've hidden Cerberus in the pet cemetery.'

'I know,' said Ned. 'Dad's the assistant part-time maintenance man here. Clever, eh? Who'd think of looking for a live animal in a cemetery?'

Ginger had to admit Ned was right. But it still seemed wrong. Poor Cerberus was facing death. How was he going to feel if he discovered he was spending the night with hundreds of pets who'd already met that fate?

Anger welled up inside her.

None of this would be happening if Mum and Dad had a bit more compassion.

'I don't know how they can do it,' she said bitterly. 'I don't know how my parents can even think about handing a dog over to be killed without proof.'

'Perhaps,' said Isabel, 'it's cause they only care about cats.'

Ginger stared gloomily at the little headstones.

'Even if you prefer cats,' she said, 'that doesn't mean you condemn an innocent dog to death. Sometimes I think Mr Napier's right, there was a mix-up at the hospital and I don't belong in that family.'

Isabel and Ned looked shocked.

'I think that's pretty unlikely,' said Isabel.

Ginger looked at her best friend's concerned face and suddenly felt a bit better. Sometimes you needed to say things even if you didn't actually believe them.

'What's more likely,' said Isabel, 'is that you're adopted.'

Ginger stared at her.

'That's right,' said Ned. 'My cousin's next-door neighbour couldn't understand why he was the only one in his family who liked cabbage. Then he discovered he was adopted.'

Ginger turned away and concentrated on wriggling through the hole under the fence.

Some people, she reminded herself, when their sleep had been disturbed, were capable of talking complete shiddle.

12

DOG NOT AROUND

'Escaped?' said Mum, pouring coffee with one hand and letting a Playground Safety Report droop in the other.

'The mongrel's gone,' said Dad, pulling his dressing-gown tighter around his tummy. 'Ripped our shed door off its hinges. We're lucky it didn't bust in here and attack us in our beds.'

Mum and Dad both looked at Ginger.

'Pet,' said Mum quietly. 'Did you hear anything last night?'

Ginger, sitting at the kitchen bench finishing her cereal, took a deep breath. If possible she wanted to get through this without lying.

'Do you mean,' she said, 'did I hear the dog ripping our shed door off its hinges?'

'Yes,' said Mum in her sternest Mrs Smith voice.

Ginger shook her head.

It was true, she hadn't. She'd removed the hinges with a screwdriver and a pair of pliers.

'When they catch that mongrel,' said Dad, 'they should give it a DNA test. I reckon they'll find it's half dingo. Or half wolf.'

Ginger didn't say anything, partly because she didn't like hearing a friend insulted like that, and partly because Dad had just given her an amazing idea.

DNA.

She knew a bit about it, but if she could find out more, it might just help her prove Cerberus was innocent.

'Well,' said Mum. 'The brute's not our problem now. Royce Napier's got the council rangers all fired up. I'm sure they'll catch it sooner or later.'

Ginger heard a meow and saw Ricebubble heading into the kitchen.

She tensed.

This was what she'd feared.

A cat desperate to spill the beans about another family member who'd snuck out of the house after midnight and hadn't got back till two-thirty.

Ginger gave Ricebubble a glare.

Don't you dare tell on me, she said silently. Not after all the cat food I gave you lot when I got back to the house last night.

She glared around at the other cats in case any of them were thinking of dobbing her in too. They didn't look like they were. Cornflake was asleep in the sink, burping softly. Cher and Kylie were dozing on the settee, stomachs hanging over the edge.

Madonna was slumped in her empty plant pot, wheezing contentedly.

Ricebubble jumped onto the bench and rubbed herself against Ginger's cheek. Ginger sneezed and nearly fell off her stool.

She couldn't believe it.

Ricebubble hadn't done that since she was a kitten, before she developed the personality of an acting principal.

'What is it, Bubblekins?' said Mum to Ricebubble. 'Are you hungry?'

The sneeze tears reminded Ginger how tired she was. She struggled not to yawn.

'Ginger,' said Mum, rattling an almost empty cat-food box. 'This was full last night. Have you been eating cat food again?'

Ginger wondered if she should say yes.

She remembered she was trying to tell the truth and shook her head.

Mum was staring at her.

'You're up and dressed very early,' said Mum. 'It's only twenty past seven.'

'I set my alarm,' said Ginger. 'In case I overslept. But I set it an hour early by mistake.'

It was the truth, and now Dad had given Ginger the DNA idea, it was extra time she could use.

For a wild moment Ginger was tempted to tell Mum the whole truth. That she was on a mission to gather evidence. A mission to save an innocent dog from an unfair death. A mission of justice.

Even in her tired state she realised that would probably be a dopey thing to do, so she settled for just part of the truth.

'I'm dropping in to Mr Wong's on the way to school,' she said. 'To see how he is and stuff.'

'Mr Wong,' said Ginger, 'what exactly is DNA?'

Mr Wong stared at her, a danish pastry halfway to his mouth.

'DNA?' he said. 'It's part of our body cells. It's what makes each person's body cells different from everyone else's.'

Ginger took a big bite of her pastry. This was sounding good.

'And animals have DNA too?' she said.

Mr Wong put his pastry back on his plate and sighed.

For a moment Ginger thought she'd asked a silly question, but then Mr Wong gave a weary nod.

Ginger was delighted, but also concerned for Mr Wong. He didn't seem his usual self. He was sort of slumped in his armchair.

Poor thing, thought Ginger. His ankle must still be hurting.

'Would you like an aspirin?' she asked, rummaging in her bag. 'I've brought the strong ones Mum uses when she has to mark maths assignments.'

'No thanks, Ginger,' said Mr Wong. He sighed again. 'It's not that sort of pain.'

Ginger was wondering what he meant as Mrs Wong came in.

'Henry,' she said, concerned. 'You haven't touched your pastry.'

'Sorry dear,' he said. 'I'm not hungry.'

Ginger was shocked. Mr Wong was always hungry. Mrs Kalinski in the tuckshop reckoned he'd eaten three jam donuts for morning tea once.

While Mrs Wong unwrapped a clean bandage, Ginger moved on to her most important question.

'If the dog that bit you left some slobber on your clothes,' she asked Mr Wong, 'could we discover which dog it was from the DNA in that slobber?'

Mr Wong nodded slowly.

'I think so,' he said wearily. 'If we had a DNA laboratory. And the dog.'

It was what Ginger had hoped to hear.

'Enough science talk,' said Mrs Wong gently to her husband. 'You've got more important things to worry about.'

Before Ginger could apologise for over-stressing Mr Wong's brain, Mrs Wong turned to her and smiled.

'Ginger,' she said. 'I'm going to change Mr Wong's bandage now. Have a look and see how much his ankle has healed in just one night.'

'I will,' said Ginger. 'But first I have to go to the bathroom.'

Ginger couldn't believe it.

A dirty washing basket without a cat inside.

She knelt on the bathroom floor and started going through Mr Wong's dirty clothes, looking for anything with dog bite marks on it.

Just one good slobber mark, she begged silently as she held a sock up to the light.

Once she found one, her mission would be half finished. Then all she'd need would be a laboratory. She'd get the lab people to show that the DNA on the clothing was different from the DNA in Cerberus's slobber, which would prove that Cerberus hadn't bitten Mr Wong.

She held some underpants up.

Nothing.

Not suprising really, she thought. Mr Wong was bitten on the ankle. The only way his undies would have dog DNA on them is if they'd fallen down mid-bite.

Ginger froze.

Somebody was tapping on the bathroom door.

'Just a minute,' croaked Ginger.

Frantically she stuffed all the dirty clothes back into the basket and unlocked the door. And saw, too late, a pair of Mrs Wong's underpants on the floor.

Mrs Wong stepped into the bathroom.

Her eyes went straight to the undies.

Then she turned to Ginger.

'I think these are what you're looking for,' she said.

Ginger blinked.

Mrs Wong was holding out a pair of grey trousers with a jagged rip in one ankle.

'The dog's jaws tore straight through them,' said Mrs Wong with a shudder. 'They're too damaged to be repaired. Take them. I hope they help you catch one of the culprits.'

Ginger took the trousers.

'Thanks,' she said. 'Thanks heaps.'

She wanted to hug Mrs Wong, but didn't because she wasn't sure what the rules were for physical contact with principals' wives.

Then what Mrs Wong had said finally sank in.

Ginger stared at her.

'What do you mean, culprits?'

'The dog that did this is only one of the culprits,' said Mrs Wong. 'The other individual that has left my husband in such a sad state is Mr Napier.'

For a crazy moment Ginger wondered if Mr Napier had bitten Mr Wong too.

Then she saw Mrs Wong was holding the local newspaper. She was pointing to a headline that said 'Principal Battles Dog Menace'. Under it was a photo of Mr Napier posing in front of the netball cage.

Ginger looked more closely.

Cerberus was in the cage.

Her chest gave a lurch, even though she knew the photo had been taken yesterday and Cerberus was safe now in the pet cemetery shed.

'Read it, please,' said Mrs Wong.

Firm but polite, thought Ginger. I wish Mrs Wong could be our acting principal.

Ginger read the news story. It was mostly an interview with Mr Napier, quoting him saying lots of things about how he was going to protect the school from the menace of stray dogs.

Then Ginger saw that Mrs Wong was pointing to one paragraph at the bottom of the page.

Ginger read it out.

The acting principal believes the danger could have been averted months ago. 'Unfortunately,' says Mr Napier, 'the previous principal did nothing about stray dogs at the school, which is why they are such a serious problem today.'

Ginger stared at the words, making sure she'd read them correctly.

She had.

'That's not fair,' she said to Mrs Wong. 'The stray dogs weren't anywhere near the school months ago.'

'You're right,' said Mrs Wong, voice shaking. 'But Mr Wong has taken Mr Napier's words to heart. He thinks he should have done something. He's torturing himself with the thought that it could have been a child who was bitten instead of him.'

Ginger gripped Mr Wong's trousers tight.

It wasn't fair. Nobody had done more for that school than Mr Wong. It was his whole life. Mrs Kalinski reckoned he even came in on Sundays to weed the Year Five Sculpture Garden and flush out the urn in the staff room.

'Mr Napier's wrong about this whole dog thing,' said Ginger. 'I'm going to prove he is. Then Mr Wong can stop feeling upset and come back to school and be our principal again.'

Mrs Wong's lips trembled and Ginger realised with a sick lurch that there was more.

'I'm afraid it's too late,' said Mrs Wong, her voice even shakier. 'Mr Wong feels he's let everyone down. He thinks it's better if someone younger steps in, someone who's better trained in school management. So he's decided to resign.'

13

ESCAPE BY A WHISKER

Ginger took Cerberus for a walk and told him the terrible news.

'Poor Mr Wong,' she said as they hurried along the street. 'I reckon he's suffering from a really serious form of depression you only get from dog bites. No offence.'

Cerberus didn't look offended.

'I reminded him how much we all love him,' continued Ginger. 'And how miserable he'd be not coming to school. And how we'd be left with Mr Napier as principal. But he was so upset he couldn't even talk about it.'

Cerberus gave a growl.

At first Ginger thought he was feeling as sick with worry as she was. Then she realised he was growling because a car was coming towards them.

'You're right,' said Ginger. 'I should be keeping a look out instead of rabbiting on.'

She wasn't sure if this was such a good idea, taking

Cerberus for a walk. But he'd looked like he needed one so much after being shut in the pet cemetery shed all night. Plus Ginger had reckoned he deserved one after the great job he'd done chewing Mr Wong's other trouser leg for a DNA sample.

It was risky. Even if the rangers weren't out and about yet, the police could be, possibly in unmarked police cars.

The car drove past without stopping.

Ginger sighed with relief and patted Cerberus, who was looking pretty relieved too.

Then Ginger saw what she was looking for.

A phone box with a Yellow Pages in it.

She explained to Cerberus that phone boxes were safer than computers because nobody could look over your shoulder and see what you were doing. She asked him to keep guard outside, stepped in and flipped through the Yellow Pages index.

Nothing.

Ginger went through the index a second time, but there wasn't a single mention of DNA laboratories.

She tried the Medical Research page.

Nothing.

She tried the Research – Industrial &/or Scientific page.

Nothing.

She was about to try the Veterinary Laboratories page, but decided to give Pathology Laboratories, whatever they were, a go first.

Yes.

DNA Testing
DNA Testing
DNA Testing

And they all gave their postal addresses.

Ginger felt breathless with excitement. If she hurried, perhaps she could post the samples off before school. She had Mr Wong's trousers in her bag, clearly marked with a big Texta V on the leg the vicious dog had attacked and a C on the leg she'd asked Cerberus to chew.

I'll need stamps, she thought. And money.

Then she heard Cerberus give another growl.

She looked outside. Another car was approaching.

Cerberus growled again, louder.

Ginger could see why. The car was a Corolla and it was exactly the same light blue as Mr Napier's.

She stepped out of the phone box to stroke Cerberus and reassure him that it wasn't Mr Napier and that she was pretty sure neither the rangers nor the police drove light blue Corollas.

Then she froze.

The car was closer now and she could see the driver's face.

Fuguggle.

It was Mr Napier.

He was looking straight at them.

Ginger grabbed Cerberus and dragged him into the phone box and pushed him onto the floor and lay on top of him, wrapping her arms and legs round him to cover as much of him as possible.

'Sorry,' she whispered. 'He must live over this way. I never knew.'

Cerberus licked her face.

Ginger squinted out through the glass.

Mr Napier wasn't stopping.

He was driving past them and away down the street.

Ginger gave a big sigh of relief into Cerberus's thick fur. 'He didn't see us,' she said. 'Quick, let's get you back to the cemetery.'

As Ginger walked across the playground, she saw other kids gawking. Most of them looked really sorry for her.

Even Locklan Grosby looked worried.

What was going on?

Isabel and Ned hurried towards her.

'Mr Napier's after you,' said Isabel, wide-eyed with anxiety. 'He saw you with the dog. Mrs Kalinski heard him telling Bruno.'

Ginger felt her insides turn to cat food.

Mr Napier must have been too scared to tackle Cerberus on his own, that's why he didn't stop. Now he'd try to force her to tell him where Cerberus was hidden, so he could send along an army of rangers.

I won't tell him, thought Ginger, gritting her teeth. Not even if he expels me.

'Go home and take a sickie,' said Ned, his long face even longer than usual. 'That's what I do when someone wants to bash me up.'

'We'll cover for you,' said Isabel. 'We'll tell him you were looking tired and exhausted, which is true.'

'And we won't say anything about dogs or sheds or pet cemeteries or anything,' said Ned. 'Not even if he tortures us with extra homework.'

Ginger looked at them both.

If things weren't so desperate she'd be feeling really good right now about having friends like them.

'Thanks,' she said. 'But he'll find me sooner or later so I might as well get it over with.'

Mrs Aljon's voice crackled out of the playground loudspeaker. 'Ginger Smith to the principal's office please. Unless she's got a good excuse for not hearing this because she's in the toilets and she's just flushed. Or she's in the tuckshop and the microwave's going. Or she's in the library standing behind a big pile of ...'

There was the loud rustle of someone else leaning over and turning the microphone off abruptly.

Ginger smiled sadly.

Even Mrs Aljon was trying to help her.

For a brief moment Ginger felt like the luckiest person in the world to be at such a wonderful school with such wonderful people.

Then a voice reminded her that she probably wasn't going to be there for much longer.

'Miss Smith,' yelled the voice. 'A moment, please.'

Ginger turned.

Mr Napier was striding towards her across the playground.

Ginger took a deep breath and tried to prepare herself for what was going to happen next.

But just before Mr Napier reached Ginger, someone grabbed his arm. It was Mrs Kalinski. She threw an anxious glance at Ginger and thrust a plate under Mr Napier's nose.

'Mr Napier,' she said excitedly. 'This is going to revolutionise fundraising. I've finally found a way of making a chocolate crackle for less than five cents. The secret is to use recycled sandwiches. Try one.'

Mr Napier looked at her icily.

'Not now, thank you, Eva,' he said.

Before he could turn to Ginger, somebody sprinted at him from the direction of the library. It was Ms Cunningham with an armful of books.

'Mr Napier,' she said breathlessly. 'I've just unpacked a new order for the teachers' resource shelf and here are some wonderful titles about Australian politics that I thought would fascinate you.'

Mr Napier looked at her even more icily.

'That's very kind, Bronwyn,' he said. 'But not now.'

Then he turned to Ginger.

'Follow me, please, Miss Smith,' he said.

As Ginger followed Mr Napier across the playground, she glanced back.

Isabel and Ned and Mrs Kalinski and Ms Cunningham were still there, watching her with worried faces.

Thanks for trying, thought Ginger.

'Wait here,' said Mr Napier.

Ginger didn't understand.

Why had they stopped outside the staff room?

Surely Mr Napier was going to interrogate her in the principal's office where he could thump the desk and where he had his phone handy to ring the rangers and the police and the local paper.

Mr Napier opened the staff room door and stuck his head in.

Ginger heard a buzz of teachers' voices.

Now she understood.

Mr Napier was going to get all the teachers to interrogate her as a team, including Mum and Dad.

'Step inside,' said Mr Napier.

Ginger thought about running for it and trying to get to the pet cemetery shed before Mr Napier or Mum or Dad or the police caught up with her, but it was too risky.

So far nobody in the staff room knew about the pet cemetery shed. It would be madness to lead them there.

Better just to let Mr Napier do what he's going to do, thought Ginger grimly, and hope I don't break down and give anything away.

She followed Mr Napier into the staff room.

14

CAT AMONG THE PIGEONS

Mum and Dad and the other teachers were sitting around the staff room table. At first they didn't notice Mr Napier and Ginger come in.

'… it was in the paper,' Ms Shapcott was saying. 'In Canada. A savage dog chewed a hole in a car.'

'In Russia,' said a Year One teacher, 'a poodle bit the head off a mountain lion.'

Ginger decided they must be in shock about Mr Wong resigning.

Everyone saw Mr Napier and went silent.

Then Ginger saw something in Mr Wong's pigeon hole. The photos and posters and certificates from his office wall. Mr Napier must have stuffed them in there. They looked so sad, all scrunched in that little space.

Suddenly Ginger felt scrunched too.

How could she stand up to all these adults? Some of them were experts at interrogation. Mum, for a start.

'Sorry to interrupt,' said Mr Napier to the teachers, 'but I know you'll be very disturbed to hear this.'

Ginger felt the eyes of all the teachers on her, including Mum and Dad.

'As you know,' said Mr Napier, 'this young lady was harassed by a stray dog on her way to school two days ago.'

Here we go, thought Ginger miserably. This is where they all try and make me tell where I've hidden Cerberus.

'This morning,' continued Mr Napier, 'this poor child was harassed by the same dog again.'

Ginger stared at him.

Harassed?

'The problem is getting worse,' said Mr Napier. 'So far this savage brute has seriously injured poor Mr Wong, escaped from custody and attacked this poor child twice. Right now it's out there somewhere, probably planning its next attack.'

Ginger was shocked. Mr Napier thought Cerberus had been attacking her. And he hadn't even stopped to help.

'This beast,' continued Mr Napier, 'may not be alone. As we know, dogs run in packs. I think this school may well be under threat from a pack of vicious stray dogs.'

Ginger felt her mouth fall open.

What was he talking about?

'My promise to you,' said Mr Napier, 'is that as

acting principal I will not run away from this problem, as I'm afraid others have done. You can count on me to marshal every available force – the police, the council rangers, the army if necessary – to protect our children and their teachers and families from this menace.'

Several teachers started applauding.

Ginger's mind was a whirl.

Did Mr Napier really think Cerberus had been attacking her? Or was he just saying that to make the dog problem seem bigger?

The teachers obviously believed everything Mr Napier had just said. They were looking at him with open admiration. Well, most of them. Mum and Dad, Ginger saw, were looking at her with deep suspicion.

I've got to tell everyone what Mr Napier's doing, thought Ginger.

Except, if she did, everyone would know about her and Cerberus.

'Ginger,' said Ms Shapcott, 'is there something you want to say?'

Ginger realised she still had her mouth open. She closed it.

'Oh, I'm sorry, Ginger,' said Mr Napier. 'I didn't mean to leave you out. Please, if you have something to say, go ahead. Perhaps something about your lucky escape this morning?'

Ginger saw the way Mr Napier was looking at her. Cocky, like he knew she wouldn't dare tell the truth.

Anger flashed through her.

'Thank you,' said Ginger. 'I just want to say …'

She hesitated.

Everybody was looking at her.

She couldn't do it. She couldn't defend Cerberus without risking his safety.

Suddenly she felt sick.

'… I just want to say,' she mumbled, 'that I was very lucky to escape this morning.'

Mr Wong was dozing in his armchair when Ginger arrived.

'Sorry to disturb you,' she said. 'But I've got something very important for you.'

She dug in her pocket and pulled out the precious document.

When she unrolled it, it looked a bit crumpled. That was the trouble with toilet rolls, poor quality paper.

'It's a petition,' said Ginger. 'Begging you to come back to school and stop Mr Napier telling lies. It's got ten signatures on it. The paw print's a dog.'

Mr Wong took the petition and stared at it.

For a second Ginger thought he was going to cry.

Then Mrs Wong interrupted. 'Ginger,' she said. 'Look, you're on the TV news.'

Ginger didn't want to look. She wished Ricebubble was here, sitting on her head so she wouldn't have to see.

But Mrs Wong turned the sound up and Mr

Wong put the petition down and peered at the TV, and Ginger found herself watching too.

There she was, on the screen, standing dejectedly next to Mr Napier in the playground.

'And this poor child,' Mr Napier was saying, 'has been attacked by vicious stray dogs not once but twice.'

I should have spoken up, thought Ginger bitterly. I should have refused to appear on camera and told them Mr Napier was talking fuguggle.

But she knew why she hadn't.

The screen cut to Mr Napier again. He was standing with the TV reporter in the Year Five Sculpture Garden.

'It's not just the brutal attacks,' Mr Napier was saying. 'These vicious strays spread disease as well. Worms. Fleas. Even headlice, I believe. Unfortunately all this started long before I became acting principal. As did these distressing examples of dog vandalism.'

Mr Napier pointed to where a chunk had been knocked out of a large polystyrene cheeseburger.

Ginger gaped. Bruno had done that accidentally with his leaf-blower.

Mrs Wong, looking like she wished she hadn't turned the sound up, grabbed the remote and the screen went blank.

'That's why you have to come back,' said Ginger to Mr Wong.

'It's a terrible thing he's doing,' said Mr Wong, looking more miserable than Ginger had ever seen a school principal look. 'But I don't know if I'm up to it. He's young and I feel so old.'

'Please,' whispered Ginger.

'Let me think about it,' said Mr Wong.

'You missed yourself on TV,' said Mitzi in the kitchen. 'We all saw it. You looked weird.'

'Thanks,' said Ginger, sneezing.

She looked down. Ricebubble was rubbing against her leg.

Typical, thought Ginger. Go on TV and everyone wants to suck up to you.

Well, not everybody.

Ginger could see Dad over in the living area trying to pull something out of Cher's mouth with both hands.

'I throw the stick,' he complained. 'She fetches it. Then she won't give it back to me.'

'Brian,' said Mum wearily. 'She's a cat.'

Dad let go of the cocktail stick and Cher ran off with it still in her mouth.

'Sometimes,' muttered Dad, 'I wonder if we'd be better off with dogs around here.'

Ginger stared at them.

I don't believe it, she thought. Mr Napier's just shown on TV what a liar he is, and all Mum and Dad can think about is cocktail sticks.

'Did you see what Mr Napier's doing?' said Ginger, going over to them. 'He's pretending there's a huge dog problem and only he can fix it so everyone will want him as principal.'

Mum and Dad looked up and saw her, and suddenly they were looking pretty outraged too. She hoped it was because they were feeling the same as her.

'Ginger,' said Mum, sounding like she'd just come back from a teachers' convention where she'd done a workshop on making her voice sound even sterner than usual. 'It's not Mr Napier's behaviour that concerns us, it's yours.'

'Did you lie to us?' said Dad. 'About the dog?'

Ginger didn't know what to say.

Was it a lie to only tell part of the truth?

'I told you he's innocent,' she said, 'and if he's caught he'll be killed for nothing and that's true.'

Mum and Dad looked at each other.

'Do you know where that dog is now?' said Mum.

Ginger took a deep breath.

It wasn't fair. All she wanted to do was protect an innocent friend. She didn't want to be like Mr Napier, but she didn't have any choice.

They were making her be a liar.

'No,' she said.

Ginger lay in bed and stared into the darkness.

How could Mum and Dad be so heartless? How could they not care that an innocent animal was facing death?

I don't get it, thought Ginger miserably. They're my parents. They shouldn't be this different to me.

Unless …

Ginger remembered what Ned had said about his cousin's neighbour and cabbage.

Am I like Ned's cousin's neighbour? she asked the darkness.

The darkness didn't answer.

Ginger knew what would happen if she asked Mum and Dad.

Mum and Dad, she'd say. Am I adopted?

She'd probably have to ask it about twenty times because Mum would be busy helping Lucrezia Funicello with her goat project and Dad would be flat out grilling Year Six about who put headlice shampoo in the boys' toilet cistern.

When she finally got Mum and Dad's attention, they'd say 'of course not, pet' and show her the photos of them holding her when she was a new baby.

Trouble is, thought Ginger sadly, I wouldn't know if they were telling the truth or not.

Everyone lies to protect the people they care about.

I lied to Locklan about Ned having a pet.

I lied to Mum and Dad about not knowing where Cerberus is.

If Mum and Dad wanted to lie to me to protect my feelings, they could easily have faked those photos.

That baby could be a dummy.

Or rented.

Ginger rolled over and pushed her face into her pillow. She'd never know, so it was a waste of time thinking about it. She decided to concentrate on what she must do to clear Cerberus's name.

First, find out how much a DNA laboratory would charge to analyse Mr Wong's trousers.

I'll do it tomorrow, she decided, as soon as I've fed Cerberus.

Ginger switched on her bedside lamp and rummaged in her schoolbag and found the page she'd torn from the Yellow Pages.

She looked at the ads for DNA labs and chose the friendliest-looking one. And saw something she hadn't noticed before. A sentence at the bottom of the ad.

'DNA Testing,' it said. 'For Parentage.'

Ginger stared at it.

She was pretty sure she knew what that meant.

DNA Testing To See If You're Adopted.

15

PROBLEM LICKED?

Ginger put the library phone down.

'Fuguggle,' she muttered.

Why couldn't people be more helpful when all you were trying to do was prove that an innocent dog was innocent and find out if your parents were really your parents?

If I ran a DNA laboratory, thought Ginger bitterly, I'd make politeness and helpfulness even more compulsory than clean test tubes.

'Are you OK?' said Ms Cunningham, coming in from the storeroom.

Ginger forced herself to look less stressed.

'I'm fine thanks,' she said. 'Somebody on the phone wasn't very helpful.'

Ms Cunningham nodded. 'I know how you feel,' she said. 'Last night Carlos tried to ring me reverse charges from Mexico and the operator put him through to Venezuela. I'll get us a chocolate milk.'

Ginger, despite the furball of anxiety in her guts,

smiled as Ms Cunningham headed for the fridge.

That was the great thing about a teacher like her. She let you use the phone on her desk without being even a tiny bit nosy. She wasn't like that bossy woman on the phone at the DNA laboratory who got angry and accused you of being a kid just because you asked for a student discount.

Ginger hunted through her schoolbag for a cough lolly. Talking on the phone in an adult voice was a real strain on your throat. She didn't know how adults managed it.

Her bag was so cluttered with DNA samples she couldn't find one.

Doesn't matter, thought Ginger. Better not tip my bag out here. Even though Ms Cunningham's very understanding, best she not see I've got Mr Wong's trousers and a scab off my knee and some of Dad's toenail clippings and a razor covered with Mum's leg hairs in my bag.

Ms Cunningham came back with two glasses of chocolate milk.

'There you go,' she said, handing one to Ginger and heading back towards the storeroom. 'Chocolate milk always makes me feel better.'

Ginger took a sip.

It was a bit spicy and it made her feel better too.

At least the DNA laboratory had told her one good thing on the phone.

They did do dog tests and parent tests.

Trouble was, when she'd asked how much the tests cost, they'd hung up.

OK, decided Ginger. I'll send them my whole life savings, including last year's birthday and Christmas money and everything I've earned cleaning out kitty litter trays for the last five years. That should be enough. I'll just keep a few dollars to buy dog food for Cerberus.

She felt even better now she'd decided that. She took a big gulp of chocolate milk, looked up at the library clock to see if she had enough time to get to the post office, and almost choked.

Coming down the corridor, peering in through the library windows, was Mum.

Oh no, thought Ginger, panic curdling the chocolate milk in her stomach. What if Mum sees me? What if she looks in my bag and sees her leg hairs?

Ginger grabbed Ms Cunningham's Mexican hat and jammed it on her head and hunched down at the desk and pretended to be Ms Cunningham looking for more books on crooked politicians for Mr Napier.

It didn't work.

'Ginger,' said Mum, coming into the library. 'I want a word with you.'

Ginger held her breath as Mum lifted the Mexican hat off her head.

She begged the leg hairs not to escape from her bag and make her sneeze.

'Pet,' said Mum softly. 'I've been worried about you.'

Ginger was so surprised she didn't know what to say. Mum wasn't being Mrs Smith, she was being Mum.

'It must have been really scary,' said Mum. 'Having that nasty brute harass you.'

Ginger nodded. She knew Mum probably meant Cerberus, but it felt better to pretend she was talking about Mr Napier.

Mum gave Ginger a long hug.

'Thanks Mum,' whispered Ginger.

Then suddenly Mum was Mrs Smith again.

'Must dash,' she said. 'Brent Bishop's grandmother's waiting to see me about his worms. Don't play with Ms Cunningham's hat unless she's given you permission.'

Mum hurried out.

This time Ginger didn't mind.

The chocolate milk inside her wasn't curdling any more, it was glowing.

Ginger looked up and down the street.

All clear.

She pulled the parcel out of her schoolbag and stuffed it into the post box. It landed with a soft thump on what sounded like a pile of other letters.

That's good, thought Ginger.

If the post box had been empty, the parcel might have split open and Mr Wong's trousers and

Ginger's knee scab and Dad's toenail clippings and Mum's leg hairs and the money order from the post office might all have got mixed up together.

Which, thought Ginger, could have totally confused the DNA people. I could have spent my entire life savings to discover that I didn't bite Mr Wong and that Mum and Dad aren't Cerberus's parents.

Instead of the way I want it to be.

That Cerberus is innocent and Mum and Dad are mine.

Ginger hurried away from the post box before somebody saw her.

When she was safely down the street, she glanced at a passer-by's watch.

Just enough time to visit Cerberus before she was due home.

I hope the delivery people are gentle with that parcel, thought Ginger as she hurried towards the pet cemetery. Perhaps I should have used another layer of bubblewrap on the toenails.

It would have been easier if she could have dropped the stuff off at the DNA laboratory in person. But after the fuss they'd made on the phone about her possibly being a kid, she hadn't wanted to risk it. Plus they'd have seen her forging Dad's signature.

Ginger decided to be like Cerberus and stop worrying.

Their futures were in the hands of Australia Post now and there wasn't anything else she could do about it.

16

BLUE HEALER

Two days.

Two days and not a single phone call from the DNA lab.

Ginger sat in the gloom of the pet cemetery shed, staring at the dead flowers on the floor.

Cerberus licked her hand.

It tickled.

'Don't,' she said.

She knew what he was trying to do. He was trying to cheer her up and it wasn't working.

Deciding to stop worrying had been easy. Doing it was much harder.

Cerberus stood up and licked her face.

'Stop it,' she said. 'I'm not in the mood.'

Cerberus looked at her, panting enthusiastically.

Ginger sighed.

'Don't you get it?' she said. 'Even if the DNA test proves you're innocent, Mr Wong's probably going to stay depressed, Mr Napier's probably going to

119

be the new principal, I'll probably be sent to a different school and you'll probably be hunted down and killed.'

The second she said it she wished she hadn't.

She put her arms round Cerberus's neck and buried her face in his fur.

She knew what he was thinking.

He was thinking she shouldn't give up. He was thinking there must be some way to get Mr Wong cheerful again. Get the old twinkle back into Mr Wong's eye. Give Mr Wong the energy to come back to school and sort Mr Napier out.

But how?

Cerberus licked her ear.

Ginger sat up and stared at him.

'Fuguggle,' she said. 'You're right. Ice skating. That used to be his favourite thing. We'll take him ice skating.'

Ginger wanted to yell with excitement. She didn't in case there was a pet funeral going on outside and she startled the vicar. Instead she hugged Cerberus as hard as she could.

'Thank you,' she said. 'You've saved us all.'

Then she had a worrying thought.

Mr Wong had a bad ankle. And he hadn't been ice skating for years. He'd probably feel pretty embarrassed doing it now in front of other people.

'No problem,' said Ginger. 'We'll hire him an ice-skating rink all to himself.'

She could see what Cerberus was thinking.

That would be expensive.

Too expensive for a person who'd just sent nearly all their savings to a DNA lab.

'Don't worry,' she said. 'I'll just have to make some money fast.'

Ginger sneezed.

She'd never run a raffle before, but it seemed to be going well.

A bit too well, actually.

The crowd of kids behind the tuckshop were getting very noisy, clutching raffle tickets and talking excitedly and pushing each other out of the way to get a peek inside Ginger's schoolbag.

'Only a dollar a ticket,' Ned was shouting to the crowd. 'Spend a dollar and get Mr Wong back as principal.'

'I think we should draw the raffle,' muttered Isabel into Ginger's ear. 'Before one of the teachers hears us.'

Ginger, wiping away the sneeze tears, agreed.

'OK,' Ginger shouted to the crowd. 'We're going to draw the raffle.'

She held up the photo of Ricebubble and pointed to her writhing schoolbag.

'Last chance to buy a ticket and win this superb pedigree long-haired Persian cat who will not only get you prizes at cat shows but also protect your house against burglars.'

'I'll have five,' said an adult voice.

Ginger froze.

Isabel and Ned gave her a nervous glance.

It was Ms Cunningham.

Except, Ginger realised with a surge of relief, Ms Cunningham wasn't being sarcastic and cross, she was smiling and holding out a five dollar note.

Ginger took it with a shaking hand and gave her five tickets.

'Let me know if I win,' said Ms Cunningham, hurrying away.

Ginger and Isabel and Ned looked at each other, blood returning to their cheeks.

'Draw the shiddleponging raffle,' hissed Isabel.

'We're drawing the raffle,' Ginger yelled to the crowd.

The crowd went quiet.

Ginger added Ms Cunningham's ticket stubs to all the others in her lunchbox, snapped the lid on, gave the lunchbox a good shake, slid her fingers in, groped for a ticket stub and pulled one out.

'B27,' she said.

The kids in front of her all studied their tickets.

Isabel gave a squeak.

'That's me,' she said, voice wobbly with panic.

Ginger stared at her.

'I don't want it,' said Isabel. 'I've got a goldfish. Finger wouldn't last two seconds with that cat.'

'In which case,' said Ginger, struggling to control her exasperation, 'why did you buy a ticket?'

'Because,' said Isabel in a tiny voice, 'I'm your friend.'

Suddenly Ginger wanted to hug her.

She didn't, partly because it would embarrass Isabel, and partly because several people in the crowd were yelling angrily.

'It's rigged,' shouted one of Locklan Grosby's mates. 'She's given it to her nurgly friend.'

'I think you'd better do it again,' muttered Ned.

Ginger agreed.

'Sorry,' she said to the crowd. 'That was a mistake. I'll draw it again.'

'Not you,' yelled another one of Locklan Grosby's mates. 'Somebody else.'

'Perhaps I could help,' said an adult voice.

Ginger froze, and this time the whole crowd froze with her.

It was Mr Napier.

'I'm always happy to help a school fundraising event,' said Mr Napier with a broad smile.

He took the lunchbox from Ginger, shook it over his head a few times, stuck his hand in and pulled out a ticket.

'B19,' he said to the crowd.

'Yes,' said a kid up the back.

'Congratulations,' said Mr Napier. He turned to Ginger. 'What's the prize?'

Ginger didn't even try to speak. She just wanted to crawl into her schoolbag with Ricebubble and stay there for ever.

But she couldn't. There wasn't room. Ricebubble, furious at being a raffle prize and even more furious at being in a bag, was thrashing about trying to claw her way out.

Mr Napier stared at the bag flopping around at his feet.

His smile turned into a scowl.

'I hope,' he said, 'that's not what I think it is.'

He bent down.

'Please,' said Ginger. 'Don't open the bag.'

Ginger stood in Mr Wong's office, waiting for Mr Napier to speak.

She guessed he probably wouldn't say anything until he'd finished putting the Band-aids on his head.

She was right.

When all five Band-aids were in place, Mr Napier turned to her.

Ginger was expecting him to be very angry. Even angrier than Mum just now when she had to leave her class and drive Ricebubble home. Even angrier than Dad the time Cornflake jumped out of the dirty washing basket and made Ginger sneeze and knock thirty-four Year Six marine biology projects into the bath.

But Mr Napier looked completely calm.

He was smiling.

Ginger realised weakly that his kitty-litter eyes, fixed unblinkingly on her, were even twinkling.

'You've blown the chance I gave you,' said Mr Napier quietly. 'As soon as I'm the new permanent principal of this school I'm going to have you transferred. And your parents. And your sister. All to different schools.'

Ginger tried to take this in. She was so dizzy with anguish she heard herself speaking before she could stop herself.

'I don't think you can do that,' she said.

'Yes I can,' said Mr Napier. 'Thanks to your criminal act in setting loose a dangerous dog that had been lawfully captured.'

Ginger stared at him.

He knew.

'And,' continued Mr Napier, 'because your sister and your parents concealed the crime.'

Ginger gawked.

What was he talking about?

'This school,' said Mr Napier, 'is a family. A very precious family. You people may not care about families and what they stand for, but I'm not going to let you destroy this one.'

'It was just me,' said Ginger. 'I set Cerberus free on my own.' She gritted her teeth. 'And I'm not telling you where he is.'

Mr Napier smiled.

'I know exactly where the brute is,' he said. 'But for now I'd rather have it roaming around the district scaring people. Now get out.'

He turned away and went back to examining his Band-aids in the mirror.

Ginger left the office, still trying to take in

everything Mr Napier had just said.

She realised she was trembling with shock and her eyes were hot and wet, even though she hadn't sneezed for at least ten minutes.

As she headed down the corridor, she made herself concentrate on the weight dragging her pockets down.

Raffle dollars.

Mr Wong ice-skating dollars.

Making-everything-OK dollars.

'One more thing, Miss Smith.'

Ginger stopped. She turned. Mr Napier was beckoning to her from his office doorway.

'The raffle money,' he said. 'Give it to me. I'm confiscating it.'

Ginger felt sick.

Run, said a voice in her head, but she didn't. Only an idiot would try and run with kilos of coins in their pockets.

Slowly she started dragging herself back towards Mr Napier.

Then somebody stepped out of the staff room and pushed past her.

It was Ms Cunningham.

'Mr Napier,' said Ms Cunningham. 'I think perhaps there's a misunderstanding here. This money has been raised to buy a present for poor Mr Wong.'

Mr Napier stared at her. Ginger stared at her too.

'I was thinking,' said Ms Cunningham, meeting Mr Napier's icy gaze, 'that this generous gesture by a student would reflect very well on the school if it was reported in the local paper.'

Mr Napier thought about this for what to Ginger seemed like the rest of the term.

Finally he spoke.

'Thank you, Ms Cunningham,' he said. 'I appreciate you fully informing me of the situation.'

Ms Cunningham grabbed Ginger and dragged her down the corridor.

'Move it,' she hissed into Ginger's ear. 'Before he changes his mind.'

'Thanks,' whispered Ginger when they were further away. 'But it's not actually for a present, it's so that Mr Wong …'

'Shhh,' said Ms Cunningham, glancing back over her shoulder. 'Don't tell me. It's better I don't know.'

Ginger understood. Ms Cunningham was new. She could lose her job with a flick of Mr Napier's pen.

Ginger glanced back too.

Mr Napier was still in his office doorway, watching them.

Ginger felt Ms Cunningham squeeze her hand.

'Whatever it is,' whispered Ms Cunningham, 'good luck.'

17

NEW LEAD

'How could you do it,' said Mum tearfully. 'How could you raffle a member of the family?'

Ginger gritted her teeth.

They weren't listening to her.

They were all just sitting around glaring at her accusingly.

Mum, Dad, Madonna, Cher, Kylie, Cornflake and Ricebubble. Even Mitzi, who was chewing her hair bunches and watching The Simpsons, was glaring at her in the ad breaks.

'I'm sorry, Ricebubble,' said Ginger. 'I did it to try and get Mr Wong back to school.'

She said it to the floor because she was having a bit of trouble looking Ricebubble in the eye.

'Mr Wong is a very nice man,' said Mum. 'He's also a wonderful principal. But Ricebubble is a member of our family.'

Mum's tears started again and she tried to give Ricebubble a hug. Ricebubble jumped away so she wouldn't get wet.

'Ricebubble still is a member of our family,' said Ginger. 'Jordan Hannagan didn't want her. When he saw what she did to Mr Napier's scalp, he tore his raffle ticket up and ran off.'

'That doesn't excuse what you did,' said Dad.

'I did it for all of us,' said Ginger. 'To stop Mr Napier taking over our school.'

Which he will do very soon, thought Ginger desperately, if I don't get started organising a very important ice-skating event.

Dad gave a Mr Smith sigh.

'I know you don't get on with Mr Napier,' he said. 'Some of the teachers feel the same. But your mother and I are senior staff members, and it's our job to support the principal, or acting principal, all the while we feel he's doing his best for the school.'

Ginger nearly exploded.

'He told me he's going to get us all moved to other schools,' she yelled.

'Ginger,' said Dad angrily. 'Stop shouting. We've been through this before. If Mr Napier said that, and I doubt it, you of all people should know that when teachers get pushed past their limit, they sometimes exaggerate a bit.'

Ginger slumped back in her chair.

It was hopeless. Why was she wasting her life savings on a DNA parent test when it was obvious that (a) she wasn't a member of this family and (b) they weren't even on the same planet as her?

Ginger dropped her plan of asking for Mum and Dad's help to find an ice-skating rink.

She got up to go.

Before she could leave, Mum went to the dresser drawer and came back with something in her hand.

'Pet,' she said, sniffing. 'I want you to look at this.'

She put a photo on the table in front of Ginger.

Ginger could hardly believe what she was seeing.

The photo was of a skinny hairless creature with a cat's face and a cat's tail. The rest of it looked more like a rat. The creature was glaring out of the photo with a mixture of anger, indignation and sadness.

I know how you feel, thought Ginger.

'Pet,' said Mum. 'This is Ricebubble's grand-mother. Her name was Ginger.'

Ginger stared at the photo. The creature didn't look anything like Ricebubble.

'She knocked an alarm clock into a can of paint and got splashed and we had to have her fur shaved off,' said Mum. 'It grew back.'

Ginger pointed at Ricebubble, who was up on a shelf trying to dislodge a placemat.

'You mean,' said Ginger, 'that under all that frizzy fur and bossiness there's one of these?' She tapped the photo.

Mum nodded.

That was mind-boggling enough, but then another thought hit Ginger and she studied the photo more closely.

If the cat was called Ginger, it must be the cat that she was …

'She died before you were born,' said Dad. 'But we named you after her because when you were a baby you often had that look on your face.'

'So in a way,' said Mum, stroking Ginger's hair, 'you're as much related to Ricebubble as you are to us.'

Ginger closed her eyes. Strange upsetting feelings were whirling around inside her and she wanted to snap out of them.

A placemat bounced off her head.

That helped.

Ginger decided to have one more go at getting Mum and Dad to listen.

'In a way,' she said, 'because our school's like a family, we're all related to Mr Wong too. Don't you care what's happening to him?'

Dad put his hand on Ginger's arm.

'Of course we do, pet,' he said. 'But Mr Wong's been teaching for nearly forty years. If you go into half the shops and businesses in this area, you'll meet people who were taught by Mr Wong. When a person's been working for that many years, it's normal to think of retiring. We shouldn't make him feel guilty about it.'

Ginger remembered Mr Wong's face the day he couldn't even manage to eat a danish pastry.

That wasn't guilt, she thought, that was sadness.

Another placemat hit her in the head.

Followed closely by a fantastic idea.

'Dad,' said Ginger. 'Has Mr Wong ever said if any of his ex-students work in ice skating?'

Dad thought about this. 'Ice skating?' he said. 'I don't know. Hang on, I think there might be one. Mr Wong told me once about a kid years ago who was so crazy about ice skating, he broke his ankle trying to skate on lino. I think he runs an ice-skating rink now.'

'Thanks Dad,' said Ginger, glowing with excitement. She rubbed her head. 'And thank you too, Ricebubble.'

The ice-rink manager gave a huge grin.

'Mr Wong?' he said. 'Best teacher I ever had. Taught me everything I know. Long division. Capitals of Europe. How to skate. Be a pleasure to see him again.'

Ginger swapped an excited grin with Isabel.

The manager scratched himself under his floppy jumper. 'I usually only open from ten till five, so any evening's fine with me.'

Ginger looked around the cavernous old wooden building. It wasn't as posh as a shopping centre rink, but there was a big oval of ice, and skates for hire, and that was all Mr Wong needed.

The manager spotted a kid eating hot chips.

'Hey,' he yelled, wobbling down the steps. 'No food on the ice unless you give me some.'

Isabel blew into her hands and rubbed them happily.

'This is perfect,' she said. 'A friendly ice rink only two bus rides from home.'

It is perfect, thought Ginger. Well, almost.

There was one more puddle to jump.

Ginger looked down at the ice and counted the people skating.

Twenty-seven. At four o'clock on a Tuesday afternoon. It didn't look like this rink was a big money earner.

Ginger hoped the manager would see it that way.

The manager was puffing back up the steps, wiping his mouth on the back of his hand. 'Little mongrel,' he said. 'I've warned him before about that. Bringing chips in here without salt.'

Ginger took a deep breath.

'How much will it cost?' she said. 'To open up for an hour one evening just for us? We've only got fifty-seven dollars.'

The manager stared at the cat-food box of raffle money Ginger was holding.

Then he shook his head.

'For Mr Wong,' he said, 'free of charge.'

Ginger couldn't believe it.

'Thank you,' she said. 'Thank you so much.'

She was still thanking him and apologising for not being able to stay for a skate because she had a hungry dog to visit, when Ned burst into the rink with a distressed look on his face.

For a second Ginger thought he was upset about being late.

Then she saw it was more serious than that.

'Ginger,' panted Ned. 'I went to feed Cerberus like you asked. But he's not in the shed. He's not anywhere in the cemetery. He's run away.'

18

DOG GONE

The shed door was flapping open and the shed was empty.

Cerberus was nowhere to be seen.

It's my fault, thought Ginger, sick with anguish. I should have got a padlock instead of relying on that stupid twist of wire.

She ran frantically around the pet cemetery, hoping, begging, pleading to see Cerberus hiding behind a gravestone or digging up a budgie.

Nothing.

'Perhaps he's gone to your place,' said Isabel. 'Or school.'

'Or the shops,' said Ned.

'Or,' said Ginger, barely able to get the words out through clenched teeth, 'perhaps Mr Napier's taken him away to be …'

She couldn't say it.

Why hadn't she moved him earlier?

Because she'd been too busy organising a dumb

ice-skating outing, that's why.

Ginger turned away.

She'd told him he'd be safe.

He'd trusted her.

Then Ginger had another awful thought.

What if Cerberus had run away because he didn't want to be with her any more?

Ginger put her hands over her face so the others wouldn't see her misery. She felt Isabel's arm creep around her shoulders. She felt Ned patting her elbow.

'Dogs can survive incredible things,' Ned was saying. 'I saw one on TV once. A plane crashed into its kennel. Luckily it was out for a walk at the time.'

Ginger wished Ned would stop. Nothing would ever make her feel better. Not even if Mr Wong came back tomorrow and Mr Napier went to live in Venezuela.

Ginger realised Isabel was tugging at her shoulder.

'Ginger,' she was saying. 'Look. What's that?'

Ginger looked.

Isabel was pointing down the street. In the far distance a dark figure was standing, watching them.

Ginger peered.

It was.

It was Cerberus.

Ginger hurled herself along the street towards him, Isabel and Ned at her heels whooping and laughing. But before she could get to him, he turned and trotted away round the corner.

'He's angry,' said Isabel. 'He's angry at us for leaving him alone so much.'

Cerberus was waiting for them halfway along the next street. As they got closer, he headed off again.

'He's making us chase after him to apologise,' said Ned. 'My dad does that to my mum after they've had a fight.'

Ginger could understand Cerberus feeling that way, yet somehow it didn't seem like him.

There he was, waiting for them in the next street and then trotting off again.

'I think,' said Ginger, 'he's taking us somewhere.'

'My feet are hurting,' complained Isabel as they stumbled over the rough ground of the building site.

Ginger's were as well, but she ignored them.

Cerberus was waiting by the half-demolished wall of an old building.

'This used to be a factory,' panted Ned. 'One of my dad's mates used to work here.'

'Come on,' said Ginger. 'Keep up.'

Cerberus disappeared into an opening at the base of the wall.

Ginger hurried over to it, crouched and peered into the darkness.

'What if it's a trap?' said Isabel.

'An ambush,' said Ned.

Ginger gritted her teeth. 'You've been watching too many horror movies,' she said.

She didn't tell them what she could smell.

Dogs.

Lots of them.

'Cerberus,' she called. 'Where are you?'

Cerberus didn't reply. Ginger could see his eyes gleaming below her in the darkness. He was waiting. He wanted her to follow. So she did.

She slid into the darkness in a shower of dust and small stones. She landed on her feet in what seemed to be some kind of cellar. She felt Cerberus lick her hand.

'I'm so glad you're OK,' she whispered, crouching and hugging his fur.

While Isabel and Ned came sliding after her, Ginger looked around.

Eyes were everywhere, gleaming.

As Ginger got used to the gloom, she saw what her nose had already told her.

'Shiddlepong,' breathed Isabel, clutching her arm. 'Hundreds of dogs.'

There weren't hundreds, Ginger saw. There were about ten. All watching her with sad dog eyes.

'So this is where the local strays hang out,' said Ginger. 'No wonder the rangers haven't been able to find them.'

'Poor things,' said Isabel. 'They look hungry.'

'They probably are,' said Ginger.

But even without looking down at Cerberus, she knew why he'd brought the three of them there.

These dogs needed more than food. They needed families.

Isabel was patting a tiny dog with big ears.

'I'm going to adopt this one,' she said. 'He's too small and nice to hurt a goldfish. Aren't you, Fang?'

Ned was being licked by a huge fat dog with short hair, very little legs and a stubby tail.

'Get off,' said Ned, alarmed.

'Don't be like that,' said Ginger, grinning. 'You'll hurt Roly's feelings.'

'All I'm asking,' said Ginger to Brent Bishop, 'is for you to adopt a dog. Just one. There are loads to choose from. All sizes.'

Brent, looking alarmed, backed away across the playground.

'Adopt a stray dog?' he said. 'No way. They're killers. Mr Napier was on TV about it. My parents reckon half of them have got rabies.'

Ginger let him go.

This is hopeless, she thought wearily. Lunchtime is almost over and I haven't found a home for a single dog.

She wondered if Ned and Isabel were having more success. Probably not. Mr Napier had brainwashed the whole school. People were avoiding her in case they got asked. She'd had to drag Brent Bishop out of the boys' toilets.

Locklan Grosby wasn't avoiding her, Ginger saw. He was heading towards her right now.

'Hey, Sneezy,' he said. 'I want to ask you something.'

Ginger didn't like the way he was glancing around furtively, as if he didn't want anyone else to see him. If he was going to insult her, why couldn't he do it out in the open like usual?

'You're a real dog-lover these days,' said Locklan, still glancing over his shoulder.

Ginger didn't say anything. No way was she offering Locklan a dog to adopt. Not after his family had sent their own dog mental. Ned reckoned it was from making it ride around in a car where the seats were covered with the skin of other animals.

'I want to do a deal,' said Locklan.

Ginger stared at him.

'What sort of deal?' she said.

Locklan stepped closer, still looking furtive.

'A dog deal,' he muttered. 'A deal to help a dog that's in big trouble.'

Ginger's mind was racing. Locklan must have found out about Cerberus. But what did he want?

Suddenly Ginger guessed. She'd seen Locklan watching her strangely during the raffle. He must have been noticing how much money she was collecting. Now he was going to threaten to tell the rangers about Cerberus unless she gave him the raffle money.

'Nurgle off,' she said.

He took another step closer to her, glancing over his shoulder again.

'You don't understand,' he said.

'Yes I do,' said Ginger. 'Get squinking lost.'

They glared at each other and Ginger wondered if Locklan was going to get violent. Then another voice spoke up behind her.

'You heard her, poonwoggle. Kronje off and leave her alone.'

It was Ned, with Isabel backing him up with her fiercest scowl.

Locklan glared at them, then walked away.

'Thanks,' said Ginger.

'He didn't look like he wanted a dog,' said Isabel.

'No,' said Ginger. 'He definitely didn't want a dog.'

'Nobody wants one,' said Isabel. 'Mr Napier's made stray dogs more unpopular than shiddle-ponging sharks around here.'

'And he's only just started,' said Ned, holding out a sheet of paper. 'We've all got to take one of these home tonight.'

Ginger read the sheet of paper.

It was a school letter to parents. Mr Napier was announcing a public meeting tomorrow night so he could tell them what he was planning to do about the stray dog menace.

'You know what this is, don't you,' said Ned gloomily. 'The latest part of Mr Napier's plan to be the new permanent principal.'

Ginger nodded. It was also, she realised with a sinking heart, the latest part of his plan to wipe out Cerberus and every other homeless dog in the district.

19

FUR REAL

'Stop it, Fang,' said Isabel. 'You mustn't do that in a phone box.'

Ginger kept the phone to her ear and sighed as Fang completely ignored Isabel.

While Isabel reached into the phone box and lifted Fang out, Ginger squeezed over to one side so her feet wouldn't get wet.

How could such a large puddle, she wondered wearily, come out of such a tiny dog?

'Bet you're glad Roly won't fit in there,' grinned Ned.

Ginger was glad. From Roly's round wobbly shape Ginger was pretty sure his body was mostly bladder.

'Come on, Mrs Wong,' pleaded Ginger. 'Answer the phone.'

Ginger could see that Cerberus, standing patiently on the dark footpath, was feeling just as stressed as her.

This whole thing was taking far too long. Buying food for ten dogs and lugging it from the supermarket to the building site had taken ages. Then, after the dogs had eaten, Isabel and Ned had insisted on taking their dogs for a walk so they didn't get fat. Or, in Roly's case, fatter.

I should have made them wait until tomorrow, thought Ginger desperately. If Mum or Dad rings Isabel's place and finds I'm not doing homework there, I'm cat food.

Mrs Wong finally picked up the phone at the other end.

'No, Roly,' yelled Ned outside the phone box. 'Don't lean on that car, you'll dent it.'

Ginger signalled frantically to him to be quiet as she said hello to Mrs Wong and asked the questions she needed to ask.

It didn't take long.

In less than a minute Ginger found out that Mr Wong was still planning to resign, that he still hadn't eaten a danish pastry, and that his foot was much better but he wouldn't be mobile enough for a surprise outing for at least a week.

Ginger agreed with Mrs Wong that it was a tjorkmin shame, said goodbye and hung up.

Mrs Wong hadn't sounded very enthusiastic about the surprise outing, so Ginger hadn't mentioned any of the details.

Like ice-skating.

Not that it mattered now.

Fuguggle, thought Ginger. Mr Napier's meeting is tomorrow night. By the time I've got Mr Wong cheered up, it'll be too late. Mr Napier will be screwing his name permanently onto Mr Wong's door.

There wasn't time to think about it now. They had to move fast.

'Come on,' said Ginger to Ned and Isabel. 'Let's get these dogs back to the building site.'

They set off down the street.

Moving fast wasn't that easy with Roly and Fang. Fang's legs were so short he was all movement and very little speed, and Roly's legs were even shorter.

Plus, Ginger saw wearily, Ned was having trouble grasping even the basic idea of moving fast.

'I've got something to show you,' he said. 'Look at this.'

'Wait till we get the dogs back,' said Ginger, but it was too late. Ned had pulled a peanut butter jar out of his pocket and unscrewed the lid.

The smell was so strong Ginger almost fainted. Only several huge sneezes stopped her.

As she pulled herself out of a hedge, she heard the dogs whimpering.

'Put the lid back on,' gasped Ginger.

Ned did.

'What is it?' croaked Ginger, wiping her eyes.

'Headlice shampoo,' said Ned. 'I invented it.'

'What with?' said Isabel. 'Nuclear waste?'

'Just stuff from the kitchen,' Ned replied, looking

hurt. 'And our shed. And some stuff they use at the pet cemetery to make dead pets smell nice. I'm going to sell it really cheaply at school, and when there's no headlice left in the whole place, everyone'll be so grateful I'll probably be school captain or something.'

Ginger stared at him.

Isabel did too.

'I got the idea from watching Mr Napier,' said Ned in a small voice. 'You know, how he's getting popular by getting rid of stray dogs. Not that dogs are like headlice.'

Before Ginger could tell Ned what she thought of people who got ideas from Mr Napier, she was dazzled by the sudden glare of headlights.

She spun round anxiously to make sure none of the dogs darted out into the road.

And saw the illuminated sign on the roof of the vehicle.

'Rangers,' she yelled at the others. 'Run for it.'

As she and Cerberus sprinted up a dark side street, Ginger was glad the others weren't with her, that they'd scattered in all directions.

That's good, she thought grimly. At least we won't all be caught.

She glanced back and saw the headlights following her into the side street.

'Look out,' she panted to Cerberus. 'They're after us.'

Cerberus veered to one side and leaped over a low

garden fence. Ginger leaped too. Cerberus snuffled and wriggled his way into a thick clump of bushes. Ginger followed. She lay on dry leaves and twigs, hugging Cerberus, silently begging the ranger truck to drive past.

It didn't.

It stopped at the kerb metres from where they were hiding.

Ginger pressed her face into Cerberus's fur as a spotlight beam cut through the foliage above her head.

'I'm sorry,' she whispered to Cerberus.

'G'day,' said a voice.

Ginger stiffened with shock.

It was a voice she half recognised.

She peered through the branches.

A kid was standing on the footpath talking to the rangers in their truck. The kid had a dog on a lead. The dog was sniffing the air and growling.

'This is Fitzherbert,' the kid was saying. 'It's OK, he's legal. If you want to come back to my place I'll show you his microchip registration and pedigree papers.'

Ginger gasped.

It was Locklan Grosby.

'Sorry to startle you, young man,' said a voice from the truck. 'Thought we saw a stray. G'night.'

The truck drove off.

Ginger couldn't believe it. What an amazing coincidence. And what unbelievably good luck. She could tell from the rapid beating of Cerberus's heart that he thought so too.

As long as the other dog didn't smell them.

'OK, Ginger,' said Locklan's voice. 'You can come out now.'

Ginger nearly wet herself. She could tell from the gurgling sounds in Cerberus's bladder that he nearly had too.

She lay there, stunned.

Cerberus stood up.

So did Ginger. Not much point skulking in the bushes if Locklan knew they were there. She followed Cerberus back to the footpath.

Locklan was watching them both with the same furtive look he'd had earlier at school.

'How did you know we were here?' asked Ginger.

'Followed you,' said Locklan.

Ginger's heart sank. Oh no. Not another attempt to bully her for money.

Cerberus must have sensed her concern, because he stepped in front of her and glared at Locklan and his dog.

Fitzherbert, a muscly little bull terrier with a mean face, growled menacingly.

'Stop that,' Locklan snapped at him. 'Another peep and you can spend the night in the car.'

Fitzherbert whimpered and backed off.

Ginger took a step closer.

'Look,' she said to Locklan. 'Me and Cerberus are

very grateful for your help, but we don't give in to extortion, OK?'

Locklan looked puzzled.

'This isn't extortion,' he said. 'I just need your advice.'

It was Ginger's turn to be puzzled.

'In return,' said Locklan, 'I've got some vital information you need.'

'What information?' said Ginger.

'First,' said Locklan, 'you have to promise you won't tell anyone about my problem.'

Ginger thought about this. She didn't trust Locklan Grosby as far as she could throw his dog. But Locklan had just saved her and Cerberus, and here he was offering to trust her.

She glanced down at Cerberus.

He looked like he thought it was OK.

'We promise,' said Ginger.

'OK,' said Locklan. 'First here's the information. My mum works for the Education Department. Remember why Mr Napier said he cancelled Pets Day? Because the student health people told him to? Well, they didn't. He was making it up. The only reason he cancelled Pets Day was because he wanted to.'

Ginger tried to digest this.

I don't get it, she thought. Why would Mr Napier cancel Pets Day when the thing he wants most is for everyone to think he's great?

Then she remembered Cornflake hanging off

Mr Napier's hair. And the rage on his face. Of course. Some people would do anything to get revenge on a cat.

'OK,' said Locklan. 'Now you have to help me. And this is top secret.'

Ginger looked at him, wondering what was coming next.

Locklan shuffled his feet and squinted at the ground.

'The dog that bit Mr Wong,' he said quietly. 'It was Fitzherbert.'

Ginger stared at Locklan. Then she stared at Fitzherbert, who scowled defiantly back at her.

'I was taking him for a walk near the school,' said Locklan, still not meeting Ginger's eye. 'A car went past, a gold Mercedes with leather seats just like Dad's, and Fitzy went ballistic. He got away from me and I ran after him and he bit Mr Wong.'

Ginger's mind was racing. This meant Cerberus was saved. But only if people knew the truth. And she'd just promised not to tell.

She saw that Locklan was watching her with a pleading look on his face. He seemed close to tears.

'I want to own up,' he said. 'I really do. But if I tell them, they might put Fitzy to sleep. You're the only other person I know who really cares about dogs. What can I do?'

Ginger didn't know what to say.

She watched Locklan crouch down and hug Fitzherbert's ugly squashed-in face to his own. It was almost as revolting as when Mum kissed Ricebubble. But deep inside Ginger knew exactly how Locklan felt.

What Ginger felt was confused.

And frustrated.

She wished she could be like Mr Napier. He wouldn't let one stupid promise stand in the way of getting what he wanted.

Ginger looked at Cerberus, and the sight of his steady gaze made her ashamed she'd even thought that.

'It's a tricky one,' she said to Locklan. 'Let me think about it. But don't worry. I won't tell.'

20

RUBBING HER NOSE
IN IT

Ginger heard Ned and Isabel's voices coming from
the cellar as she picked her way across the dark
building site.

'They're OK,' she said to Cerberus, her insides
wobbly with relief. 'They must have got away from
the rangers.'

Cerberus's panting sounded pretty relieved too.

Ginger couldn't wait to tell Ned and Isabel the
three-part plan she and Cerberus had been working
on since they'd left Locklan.

Part One, let everyone at Mr Napier's meeting
know that Pets Day was OK with the Education
Department. Once everyone knew, Mr Napier
would have to agree.

Part Two, take Cerberus and Fang and Roly to
Pets Day, so everyone could see how well-behaved
and polite and gentle stray dogs could be and how

Mr Napier was wrong about them.

Part Three, take Mr Wong ice-skating so he'd get his confidence back and cheer up and be school principal again.

Ginger grinned.

Ned and Isabel are going to be so excited when I tell them, she thought happily.

She followed Cerberus into the opening at the base of the wall.

As soon as Ginger slid into the cellar and flashed her torch around, she saw something was wrong.

The other dogs were lying on the rubble, miserable and silent. So were Isabel and Ned. Isabel looked like she'd been crying. Ned's face was longer than Ginger had ever seen it.

'They caught Roly,' he said quietly. 'The rangers caught Roly.'

Ginger didn't hesitate. She pulled Ned and Isabel to their feet. 'Come on,' she said. 'If we go straight to the ranger depot we can get him back. We'll explain that Roly belongs to Ned and that Ned was planning to register him tomorrow.'

Isabel sat down again.

'We've already tried that,' she said. 'They said they wanted to help but they couldn't give him to us. They said they had to keep him for someone else.'

'Who?' said Ginger.

Isabel and Ned both looked at Ginger with bleak faces.

'Mr Napier,' said Ned. 'The rangers reckon Mr

Napier's going to put Roly on display at his public meeting tomorrow.'

The hall was packed.

Parents mostly, Ginger could see as she turned round in her seat. Some teachers too, and kids.

Mum and Dad were up the back, deep in conversation with a couple of parents.

Probably just explaining to them what a good job Mr Napier's doing, thought Ginger gloomily.

On either side of her, Ned and Isabel were peering anxiously up at the stage.

'I can't see Roly,' said Ned.

'Perhaps the rangers were joking,' said Isabel.

Ginger doubted that rangers were allowed to joke in uniform. True, the stage was empty except for a lectern and a couple of chairs, but that was only because the meeting hadn't started.

Then the meeting started.

Locklan's father, the President of the School Council, took his place on the stage and introduced Mr Napier, who walked on to loud applause.

Ginger didn't want to look like a trouble-maker too early so she pretended to applaud, but didn't let her palms actually touch.

She slid forward onto the edge of her seat, heart going even louder than the clapping.

The moment wasn't far away now.

The moment to speak out.

'Thank you all for coming,' said Mr Napier.

'These are worrying times for our school. I can tell from your faces you agree. And I can tell you also agree that at times like this we require strong leadership.'

Now, thought Ginger. Before he gets onto the dog scare stuff. Tell them about Pets Day now.

Ginger was halfway to her feet when Mr Napier broke into a big smile.

'First,' he said, 'some good news. As you know, after the brutal attack on Mr Wong, the Education Department said no to Pets Day. That upset me greatly. I know how much Pets Day means to our children. So I went back to the Department and urged them to think again, and I'm delighted to announce that they've just said yes to Pets Day.'

The hall erupted into even louder applause and cheering.

Ginger sat down, stunned.

What was going on?

Was Mr Napier telling the truth? Had Locklan's mum got it wrong?

Isabel, also looking stunned, grabbed Ginger's arm. 'Locklan must have got his shiddleponging facts back to nurgling front,' she said.

Ginger looked up at Mr Napier, who was glowing as the applause continued and was smiling even more widely.

Suddenly she knew.

'No,' she said. 'Mr Napier planned this.'

Ginger wanted to stand up so much her teeth were itching. She wanted to stop the applause and tell everyone the truth. That Mr Napier had faked the whole thing to make himself look like a hero.

But she didn't.

She gritted her teeth and thought of Cerberus. And the other dogs. And how important Pets Day was going to be for them.

They've got their chance now, she told herself. Don't risk losing it again.

Mr Napier's smile vanished and he held up his hands. The applause died away.

'I wish all the news was good,' he said. 'But it's not. This school is in danger. Violence lurks in our community. Threatening us and our children. In the past, nothing was done to fight back. Well, I've changed that. Now we are fighting back.'

Mr Napier signalled to somebody behind the curtain at the side of the stage.

Suddenly Ginger knew what was coming next.

She could tell Ned did too because he grabbed her arm.

People around the hall gasped as Bruno appeared with a dog on a lead. The dog's stumpy legs were trying to resist, but even the weight of his wobbly body wasn't enough to prevent Bruno dragging him onto the stage.

'Roly,' whispered Ned.

Ginger gasped too. Bruno's right arm was bandaged and in a sling. She knew everyone would think Roly had done that. Instead of Bruno falling off a pogo stick or something.

'Only last night,' said Mr Napier, 'this brute was at large in the community.'

Ginger hoped people would think he meant Bruno, but she was pretty sure they wouldn't.

'I said to myself,' continued Mr Napier, 'enough. No more. This has got to stop.'

Mr Napier gave the lectern a dramatic thump.

As his arm came down, Roly whimpered and tried to hide behind Bruno's legs.

'Mr Napier's scaring him,' said Ned.

Ginger could see Ned was right.

Poor Roly must have been hit as a puppy, she thought, and now any thumping at all makes him upset.

'Don't confuse these mongrels with the dogs you love and trust at home,' said Mr Napier, pointing angrily at Roly. 'Don't ever trust one of these brutes, because they don't know the meaning of love.'

He thumped the lectern again.

'No,' whimpered Ned.

Ginger could see Roly's whole body was trembling with fear and stress.

'These mongrels,' said Mr Napier, 'don't even know who their parents are. They're vicious and angry because they know they'll never amount to anything.'

Ginger realised her whole body was trembling too.

Not with fear, with fury.

'That's why they hate us,' continued Mr Napier, thumping the lectern yet again. 'That's why they must be wiped out.'

He gave the lectern a final big thump.

Suddenly Ginger saw that Roly wasn't cowering any more. Suddenly he was hurtling through the air at Bruno.

Ginger couldn't believe it. How could legs that short get a body that size off the ground?

Bruno crashed backwards onto the stage with Roly on his chest.

Roly grabbed the lead in his mouth and tore it out of Bruno's hand.

Mr Napier was cowering now, trying to hide his whole body behind the lectern. But Roly wasn't interested in Mr Napier. Eyes even wider and more fearful than Mr Napier's, he made a dash for freedom down the stage steps and towards the doors at the back of the hall.

Ginger saw the problem immediately.

The hall was full of people yelling and screaming and climbing on chairs. The doors were shut. Roly would be trapped. Sooner or later somebody would have a go at picking up a chair and bashing Roly with it.

Ginger jumped up and went after Roly.

People were flinging themselves out of his way as he scampered towards the back of the hall, dragging the lead behind him.

Ginger saw Locklan Grosby frozen, not sure whether to help or hide. His mates were scrambling under chairs. Little kids were clinging to their parents' legs like kittens hanging off furniture. Other parents were in each other's arms or the arms of teachers.

Ginger stayed as close to Roly's tail as she could. Suddenly they were almost at the doors.

Only two people blocked the way.

Mum and Dad.

They were rigid with terror, as if they expected Roly to leap up and bite them in the throat.

Ginger flung herself between them and let her whole body crash into the locking bar on the inside of the doors.

The doors swung open. Roly hurtled past Ginger and out of the hall. Ginger watched his little legs blur as they carried him across the playground. She waited till he was out of sight down the street, then turned to face Mum and Dad and the chaos in the hall.

Mum and Dad were looking at her with dazed expressions.

'Pet,' said Mum, a quiver in her voice. 'You saved us.'

The rest of the meeting seemed to take weeks.

Once all the chairs were back in rows and people were seated again, Mr Napier called Ginger up onto the stage.

She had to sit there while Mr Napier told the

audience that what they'd just witnessed proved how serious the whole dog threat was.

He then told them how Ginger had been attacked twice by vicious stray dogs, and how the shock had changed her from a model student into a tragic case who was having trouble remembering even the simplest rules of reasonable behaviour.

Ginger managed to control herself.

She also managed to control herself when Mr Napier went on to say how, thanks to him, no other child would suffer what Ginger had suffered because every vicious stray dog in the district would soon be a thing of the past.

Finally Ginger managed to control herself one more time when the president of the School Council thanked Mr Napier and told the audience that following the resignation of Mr Wong, the School Council Appointments Committee would be recommending Mr Napier as the new permanent school principal.

Ginger didn't yell anything out.

She didn't even cry.

She just sat quietly thinking about the thing that was going to save Cerberus and the others.

Pets Day.

21

RAINING CATS AND LIZARDS

The moment Ginger and the others walked under the Pets Day banner and into the crowded playground, every human and animal eye was on them.

Ginger wanted to run, but she didn't.

In the cat enclosure, Ginger could see, most of the cats wanted to run too. The others were thinking about climbing up the Pets Day banner.

'It's OK,' she murmured to Cerberus. 'If they go for Mr Napier's head, it's their problem, not yours.'

Ginger could see Cerberus agreed.

She could also see that every eye in the playground was still on her and Isabel and Ned and the three dogs trotting at their heels.

The humans were mostly open mouthed. So were most of the lizards. The budgies, parakeets and lovebirds were blinking frantically. The mice, rats and guinea pigs were twitching nervously. Quite

160

a few parents and teachers were blinking and twitching as well.

When Ginger reached the middle of the playground, she signalled to Ned and Isabel to stop. The mixture of smells swirling around was making her head spin.

It must be even worse for the dogs, she thought anxiously.

She crouched down next to Cerberus's ear.

'Be brave,' she whispered, 'and good.'

Ned and Isabel were doing the same with the other dogs.

Ginger stood back up as tall as she could.

'Everyone,' she said to the gawking teachers and kids and parents and pets. 'This is Cerberus and Roly and Fang. I hope you'll make them welcome, because they're our pets.'

'And we love them just as much as you love your pets,' said Isabel. 'And my other pet.'

'And they're not the vicious brutes some people say they are,' said Ned. 'We've brought them here so you can see for yourselves.'

There was a nervous twittering, squawking, meowing, growling, splashing and bleating from the assembled cages, boxes, baskets, bowls, trailers and humans.

One of Locklan's mates was staring nervously at Roly.

'That's not a Peruvian tree spider,' he squeaked indignantly to Ned.

Cerberus, Roly and Fang stood rock still.

Ginger swapped a proud look with Isabel and Ned. All the practice they'd done in the cellar about not panicking and getting over-excited was paying off. For them and the dogs.

Then Joe O'Reilly's little white terrier ran over and sniffed Roly's bottom.

Ginger sent a silent plea to Roly to remember what he'd learned at rehearsals.

No snarling.

No biting.

No sitting on little dogs and squashing them.

Ginger saw she needn't have worried. Roly was the perfect gentleman. He let the little dog sniff for the polite amount of time, then took his turn sniffing the little dog's bottom. He even managed to look as though he was genuinely interested in the smell.

'What well-behaved dogs,' said a voice.

Ginger looked round.

It was Ms Cunningham. She came over and patted Cerberus, and then Roly, and then Fang.

Please, Ginger begged the dogs silently. Please remember what we said yesterday. If you're going to bite anyone, please make sure it's not a teacher.

Nobody bit Ms Cunningham.

'I can't officially say I approve of what you've done,' said Ms Cunningham to Ginger, Ned and Isabel. Then she leaned forward and whispered into Ginger's ear. 'But I admire you a lot.'

Ginger glowed.

That felt really good coming from a woman who'd had library books chewed by dogs.

'Would you like a chocolate crackle?'

Mrs Kalinski appeared carrying a plate.

For a second Ginger thought Mrs Kalinski was asking her. Then she realised Mrs Kalinski was offering the plate to Cerberus.

Cerberus looked a bit taken aback.

'I'm not sure if he likes them,' said Ginger.

'Roly does,' said Ned. 'Thanks.' He took one and Roly gobbled it up.

Several other kids pushed forward, letting Mrs Kalinski know that their pets liked chocolate crackles too.

'A tortoise?' Ginger heard Mrs Kalinski say. 'Are you sure?'

Ginger felt someone tugging at her sleeve. She looked down. It was Mitzi, clutching a grumpy-looking Cornflake.

Ginger was glad she'd taken extra sneeze tablets.

'Mum and Dad'll kill you,' said Mitzi. She pointed across the playground to where Mum and Dad were hurrying towards them.

'Ginger Smith, stay right where you are,' roared a voice.

For a moment Ginger was confused because the voice came from the opposite direction, but when she spun round she saw why.

It was Mr Napier.

Bruno was trotting behind him, arm still in a sling.

'You just won't learn, will you?' said Mr Napier to Ginger. He turned to Bruno and pointed to Cerberus, Roly and Fang. 'Grab those dogs.'

Bruno looked uncertain.

Ginger knew why. Hanging on to just Roly with a dud arm had been hard enough for Bruno. Three dogs was going to be impossible.

Ginger realised Mr Napier was putting his face close to hers. Everyone was watching. She hung on to Cerberus's neck fur, praying he wouldn't go for Mr Napier and ruin everything.

She saw Mr Napier realise everyone was watching too.

'Ginger, Ginger, Ginger,' said Mr Napier, trying to smile. Hate poured from his eyes like cat vomit. 'I've said this before and I'll say it again. How your parents ended up with a little criminal like you I do not know.'

Ginger shifted her eyes away from Mr Napier's so her brain wouldn't explode and she wouldn't be tempted to try and bite his nose off.

For a brief moment her eyes met Mum and Dad's. They were looking shocked.

Then Ginger was startled by Mr Napier making a sudden movement. He reached into the crowd and grabbed something. It was a dog lead. Mr Napier dragged it towards him. On the other end was Fitzherbert. Close by was Locklan, looking terrified.

'Before I expel you,' Mr Napier said to Ginger, 'I want to give you one last lesson at this school. I want to teach you the difference between a pet and a pest.'

Ginger watched him grin at the crowd, waiting for them to appreciate his witty way of putting it. Nobody seemed to be that amused.

Mr Napier pointed to Cerberus, Roly and Fang.

'That,' he said, 'is trash. It has no place in our school. I decide who and what comes through our gate. The likes of that will never set foot in our school again.' He glared at Ginger. 'And neither will you.'

Ginger hung on to Cerberus.

Ned and Isabel were doing the same to Roly and Fang, who were both looking at Mr Napier as if he'd taste very good indeed.

'This,' said Mr Napier, pulling the lead and jerking Fitzherbert closer to him, 'is a quality animal. You can tell just by looking at him. Quality breeding, quality training and quality family.'

There was a smell nagging at Ginger's nose. A smell similar to, but different from, all the other animal smells swirling around her.

Suddenly she realised what it was.

Leather.

Mr Napier, she saw, was wearing leather gloves. He must have put them on because he knew he'd be handling animals at Pets Day.

Ginger saw another nose react to the leather

smell. Fitzherbert's. The ugly dog didn't like it at all. Ginger remembered how much Fitzherbert hated leather car seats.

'You can see the intelligence in the eyes,' Mr Napier was saying, pointing to Fitzherbert's head. Fitzherbert was struggling to get away. Mr Napier grabbed him and tried to turn his squashed-in face towards Ginger and the others.

Fitzherbert gave a desperate howl, wriggled out of Mr Napier's hands, flopped onto his back, flipped over onto his feet, and sank his teeth into Mr Napier's ankle.

'Fitzy,' yelled Locklan. 'Not again.'

Mr Napier screamed and staggered back, still with Fitzherbert attached to him. He crashed into Emily Cummins's ant farm, which toppled over. Several million ants made a run for it. Most of them into Trav Scott's box of rats.

Trav yelled as ants ran up his arm.

Ginger tried to stop the rat box tipping over but she was too late and rats swarmed among the people and pets.

Shaun Blake's yellow-spotted miniature frill-necked lizards bolted.

Leah Pobjoy's parakeet flew into Christina Mercuri's guinea pig box and the terrified guinea pigs threw themselves over the edge.

People yelled and screamed.

Ms Shapcott tried to keep the lizards off her by squirting them with skin moisturiser.

Bruno tripped over a sheep and fell face forward into an inflatable paddling pool full of frogs.

More pet containers were knocked over.

Pets, finding themselves suddenly free, panicked and didn't know what to do. Some of them decided to try and run home. Others decided to move to Queensland.

People chased animals.

Animals chased people.

Suddenly Ginger was one of the only people not moving in a playground full of mayhem. Ned, she saw, was one of the others. And Isabel. They were both staring, stunned, at everything going on around them.

Cerberus was growling at Roly and Fang. For a horrible moment Ginger thought he was urging them to join in the chaos.

She realised she should have known better.

The three dogs stood their ground, flinching occasionally when another panicked animal whizzed past very close.

Pets were swarming all over the school grounds and out into the street. Parents and teachers were chasing after them and yelling at kids to stay inside the fence.

Mum and Dad rushed past, trying to reach Lucrezia Funicello who was being dragged around the playground on her bottom by her hysterical goat.

Ms Cunningham and Locklan were trying to

prise Fitzherbert's jaws off the howling Mr Napier's ankles with a ruler.

Nobody, Ginger realised sadly, was noticing what well-behaved, polite and gentle dogs Cerberus, Roly and Fang were.

And it'll get worse, she thought. In a few hours, when the chaos is under control and all the pets have been caught, everyone will probably blame us.

Part two of the three-part plan hadn't gone so well.

Ginger grabbed Ned and Isabel.

'Take the dogs back to the cellar,' she said. 'I'm off to Mr Wong's.'

There was only one thing left now that could save Cerberus and the other dogs and the future of the school.

Mr Wong's surprise outing.

22

WHAT'S NEW PUSSYCAT?

'A surprise outing?' said Mr Wong, staring at Ginger
as if she was mad.

Ginger nodded and tugged at Mr Wong's sleeve.
If she could just get him off his front door step and
into a taxi, everything would be OK.

Probably.

'That's very kind, Ginger, but it's not a good time,'
said Mr Wong, peering up and down the street. 'The
whole district's full of escaped animals. I should
have given Mr Napier better instructions on how to
run Pets Day. The least I can do is help catch some
of the pets.'

An armadillo ran past the front gate, chased by
two little kids and a puffing teacher.

'It's OK, Mr Wong,' said Ginger desperately.
'They'll be fine. They've got a butterfly net.'

Mrs Wong grabbed Mr Wong's arm.

'Don't even think about it, Henry,' she said. 'Your
ankle's in no condition to be chasing reptiles.'

'An armadillo's not a reptile,' said Mr Wong sulkily.

'And I don't want you sneaking off while I'm out,' added Mrs Wong. 'I've just promised to drive Mrs Cloony and her cat to the vet. Fluffy has just eaten part of a yellow-spotted frill-necked lizard.'

Mrs Wong bit her lip and Ginger could see she was worried about what Mr Wong would get up to while she was away.

'If Mr Wong comes with me,' said Ginger, 'I promise he won't do any running or chasing.'

She gave Mr Wong an apologetic look. Sorry, she tried to tell him silently, but I promise you'll have fun anyway.

'Henry,' said Mrs Wong, 'I think you should go on the outing with Ginger. It would be awful to disappoint her after all the planning she's put into taking you to the ... er ... where is it exactly, Ginger?'

'It's a surprise,' said Ginger.

Mr Wong thought about this for what felt to Ginger like hours. Then, just when Ginger had given up all hope, she saw a twinkle in Mr Wong's eyes.

She hoped it wasn't just the reflection of the flashing light on the ranger truck that was passing.

'All right,' said Mr Wong, limping off down the hallway. 'I'll get my jacket.'

Ginger wanted to hug Mrs Wong, but before she could, Mrs Wong stepped closer and spoke in a quiet voice.

'Don't worry, I'm not going to make you tell me where you're taking him. A surprise is a surprise. It may not be good for his ankle, but let's hope it'll be what the rest of him needs.'

'I think it will be,' said Ginger.

'All I ask,' said Mrs Wong, 'is have him home by ten o'clock.'

In the taxi, Mr Wong wasn't quite as excited as Ginger had hoped he would be.

'Do I have to wear this blindfold?' he said. 'It's very itchy.'

'Sorry,' said Ginger. 'It's so you'll be surprised.'

She wished she'd had something better than one of Ned's footy socks.

'If I can guess where we're going,' said Mr Wong, 'I'm allowed to take it off.'

Ginger didn't reply. When a principal set his mind on something, there wasn't any point arguing.

'McDonald's,' said Mr Wong.

'No,' said Ginger.

'The movies,' said Mr Wong.

'No,' said Ginger.

'The Chinese calligraphy exhibition at the State Library,' said Mr Wong.

'No,' said Ginger.

She was starting to wonder if ice skating was such a good choice after all. And she could do without this extra stress, because there was something else that was worrying her so much her insides felt like she'd swallowed an armadillo.

It was what she'd seen as she was leaving the chaos in the school playground.

Mr Napier, hobbling into his car with a murderous expression on his face.

Ginger couldn't stop thinking about where he was off to, and whether it would involve danger to Cerberus.

'Not yet,' said Ginger as Mr Wong started to take the blindfold off.

She finished paying the taxi-driver with the raffle money, then helped Mr Wong out of the taxi.

Ginger took a deep breath.

'Now,' she said.

Mr Wong took off the blindfold. He stared blinking at the old wooden ice-rink building and at his old pupil the manager, who was standing on the steps scratching himself happily.

Ginger knew this was the moment of truth.

Either Mr Wong would like the idea, or he'd be plunged into depression that it wasn't the State Library and get back into the taxi and go home and leave Mr Napier to ruin everyone's lives.

'Gavin,' said Mr Wong, beaming. 'Gavin Pilger.'

'G'day Mr Wong,' said the manager, holding out a pair of ice skates. 'Your size, I believe.'

23

NO PAL

Ginger watched Mr Wong glide across the ice like an elderly swan.

Wrinkled but graceful.

Ginger felt very relieved.

Getting the skate on Mr Wong's sore foot had been a bit tricky, but once Mr Wong set his mind on it, nothing was going to stop him.

If he was in pain now, he wasn't showing it. Ginger had never seen him look so happy.

It's working, thought Ginger, tingling with happiness herself.

'Mr Wong,' called the manager with a cheery wave. 'I'm off now. Got a night job at an iron foundry. Saving up to take the wife skating in Switzerland.'

Mr Wong waved back without interrupting his double reverse pirouette.

'Thanks, Gavin,' he called. 'I'd like to do this again soon.'

'My pleasure,' said the manager.

He turned to Ginger.

'When you leave,' he said, 'just pull the door shut. It'll deadlock automatically. Oh, and turn the lights off with that switch there.'

'OK,' said Ginger.

'Don't touch the red dial,' said the manager. 'That controls the temperature for freezing the ice, but I've got it on automatic.'

'OK,' said Ginger. 'Thank you so much. You've just saved a school and about ten dogs.'

'Glad to help,' said the manager, and was gone.

Ginger sat watching Mr Wong curve and glide across the ice, smiling and waving to her often, on one foot sometimes.

Good thing he's so skilled, she thought, waving back. Means he can give his sore ankle a rest.

She decided that once Mr Wong was back at school, she was going to ask him if they could do ice skating as a school subject. That and pet grooming. Which would have the added advantage that when Mr Napier found out, he'd probably put in for a transfer to another school.

Ginger's stomach knotted.

She wished she hadn't thought about Mr Napier.

Then she heard panting. For a second she thought Mr Wong had been overdoing it on the ice. But when she looked up she saw something that made her leap to her feet.

Cerberus bounding towards her over the seats.

Followed by Roly and Fang.

And, she realised, as she stared in alarm at the commotion in the doorway, all the other dogs from the building site cellar.

'What's happened?' she asked Cerberus as all the dogs clamoured round her, licking her and barking. 'Where are Ned and Isabel?'

Cerberus was barking too. He was so agitated Ginger couldn't understand what he was trying to tell her.

'What's wrong?' she said. 'Has something happened to Ned and Isabel?'

Mr Wong skated to the edge of the rink, looking alarmed too.

'Are you all right?' he called to Ginger. 'Do you know these dogs?'

Before Ginger could explain that she did, Ned and Isabel came sprinting in.

The dogs fell silent.

'It's Mr Napier,' said Isabel, wild-eyed and gasping for breath. 'He was waiting for us at the building site in his car. He knows about the dogs. When we saw him we ran for it. The dogs all came here.'

She was out of breath. Ned, who was looking very distressed himself, took over.

'The dogs led us down back alleys and cut across gardens but Mr Napier tracked us in his car. He'll be arriving any minute. We've got to get the dogs out of here.'

'Too late,' said a familiar voice.

Ginger didn't want to look but everyone else did so she had to.

In the doorway was Mr Napier. His ankle was bandaged and he was using a blackboard pointer as a walking stick.

'Royce,' said Mr Wong, amazed. 'What are you doing here?'

'Something I should have done a long time ago,' said Mr Napier.

Balancing on one foot, he swung the door shut with a clang.

Ginger groaned.

So did Cerberus.

Mr Napier looked at Ginger with narrowed eyes.

'You'd better tell your furry friends to prepare for the worst,' he said. 'When this many strays are caught all at once, the pound officials don't even waste time trying to get them adopted.'

Ginger felt Cerberus stiffen next to her.

Mr Napier pulled out a mobile phone and dialled. 'Give me the ranger depot,' he said. 'It's Napier. I've found the dogs. You'll need two trucks and at least a dozen tranquilliser darts. The address is …'

Then he shook the phone and swore at it.

Even though Ginger was in shock, she noticed his swearwords were a lot less original than the ones most people at school used.

Mr Napier glared at them all.

'Don't think you're getting away,' he said. 'I've got another phone battery in the car.'

He turned and tried to open the door.

He couldn't.

'It's deadlocked,' said Ginger.

'Rubbish,' said Mr Napier. 'Don't lie to me. I know how this technology works.'

Before Ginger could shout a warning, he reached up and turned the red dial.

'That's not the door lock,' yelled Ginger.

Mr Napier ignored her. When the door didn't open he turned the dial the other way. Then several times more in both directions.

The lights went out.

'That's the temperature control,' said Ginger. 'Touching it must affect the lights.'

'As well as lower the temperature by the feel of it,' said Mr Wong, walking up from the ice.

'Rubbish,' said Mr Napier again. He flicked the light switch about fifty times. The lights stayed off.

Ginger shivered. Mr Wong was right. It was getting colder. All their breaths, humans and dogs alike, were gleaming white in the moonlight spilling down from the tiny windows high above them.

Mr Wong tried to turn the temperature back up again, but no amount of fiddling with the dial made the air get anything but colder.

'The manager said something about an automatic system,' said Ginger. 'It must be jammed.'

Mr Wong turned his attention to the door. No amount of fiddling with that made it anything but locked.

'Looks like we're stuck here till someone comes to let us out,' said Mr Wong. 'Who has somebody who knows they're here? Ginger, what about your parents?'

Ginger shook her head, not wanting to meet Mr Wong's eye.

'Mine don't know I'm here either,' said Isabel in a tiny voice. 'Nor does Finger.'

'Nor do mine,' said Ned.

'I'm not sure if Mrs Wong knows I'm here or not,' said Mr Wong. 'But even if she does, she's not expecting me till ten. She also knows how young people can forget the time, so she probably won't get alarmed till at least eleven.'

That means we might not be rescued till after midnight, thought Ginger. We could be frozen to death by then.

She realised Mr Wong had forgotten to ask Mr Napier.

'Mr Napier,' she said. 'Do you have anyone who knows you're here?'

Mr Napier didn't answer.

'No, Ginger,' said Mr Wong softly. 'Mr Napier doesn't. He's not married and he hasn't got a family and judging by some of the things he's been doing to people lately, I'd say he probably hasn't got any friends either.'

Mr Napier glared angrily at Mr Wong, but Ginger saw something else in his eyes too. A look a cat gets when you're five minutes late feeding it.

Furious, but underneath very hurt.

Ginger stared at Mr Napier, trying to imagine what it would be like to have no family and no friends either.

She shivered, and not just because the air was getting colder.

24

HOT DOGS

Ginger was getting more and more worried about Mr Wong.

They were all sprawled out on the ice-rink seats, exhausted from walking around and slapping their arms for so long. Mr Wong was shivering badly in his thin shirt and looking pale in the moonlight.

'Are you sure you don't want my T-shirt?' Ginger said to him. 'I've got a singlet on underneath.'

'Or,' said Isabel, 'you can have my tank top and I'll have Ginger's T-shirt.'

'Take my shirt,' said Ned. 'I don't need anything.'

Mr Wong smiled through chattering teeth.

'You're all very kind,' he said. 'But I'll be fine.'

'You heard him,' snapped Mr Napier from his seat. 'Give it a rest.'

I don't reckon he will be fine, thought Ginger anxiously. It's OK for us younger ones, we've got better blood circulation and we're used to not wearing enough clothes. And Mr Napier's OK because angry people always stay warmer. But Mr Wong's old and nice. That could be fatal.

Ginger tried to think of something to save Mr Wong.

Cerberus and the other dogs had already sniffed every centimetre of the ice rink looking for another way out.

There wasn't one.

Ginger and Isabel and Ned had already tried throwing ice skates up to break the glass in the tiny windows to let some warm air in, but they couldn't even get the skates high enough. Plus a falling skate had nearly chopped Mr Napier's blackboard pointer in half.

Ginger couldn't think of another thing they could do.

She sighed in despair, billowing out frozen breath.

Cerberus came over and nuzzled his warm face into her cold hands.

His very warm face.

Ginger stared at him.

'Cerberus,' she whispered. 'Do you think you could keep Mr Wong warm?'

She could tell from his eyes that he could, and that he thought it was a good idea.

'Mr Wong,' she said. 'Come and lie down and let Cerberus keep you warm.'

Mr Wong looked doubtful at first, until Ned reminded him that Antarctic explorers had survived blizzards heaps of times by cuddling dogs.

Lucky this is an old rink, thought Ginger as Mr Wong lay down on the wooden floorboards of the viewing area. In a modern rink this would be freezing tiles.

Cerberus lay down and snuggled into Mr Wong. So did Roly and Fang. Before Ginger could ask the rest of the dogs, they all came and did the same.

'This is beautifully warm,' said Mr Wong. 'Come on, there's plenty of room for everyone.'

He's right, thought Ginger once she and Isabel and Ned had snuggled in with Mr Wong and the dogs. If more people had dogs instead of cats, houses wouldn't need central heating.

'Come on, Mr Napier,' she said. 'There are enough dogs for you too.'

Mr Napier huddled in his seat and scowled at her.

'Lay down with strays and no hopers?' he said through chattering teeth. 'No way.'

Ginger was drifting in and out of sleep, dreaming that the DNA test results showed she was actually the daughter of Ms Cunningham and Carlos, so at first she wasn't sure what the sound was.

It was different from the other sounds. From the soft wheeze of sleeping dogs. From Mr Wong's gentle snoring. From the distant hum of the freezing units.

Ginger lifted her head carefully so as not to disturb any of the people or dogs huddled around her.

On the far side of the huddle she saw, in the moonlight, a blackboard pointer on the floor. Lying next to it, between two large dogs, was Mr Napier.

His face was buried in the furry flank of one of the dogs, and his shoulders were moving up and down.

Ginger realised the sound was coming from him.

It was such an unhappy sound, Ginger could hardly bear to listen.

Ginger woke with a jolt.

Warm air was flowing over her face. For a second she thought it was Cerberus's breath. Then she heard voices and realised the ice-rink door was open.

People were crowding in.

Ginger sat up and gasped with relief.

It was Mum and Dad. And Mrs Wong. And Ned's and Isabel's parents. And Mr Grosby. And the ice-rink manager. And quite a few people she didn't recognise because she had sleep in her eyes.

The whole group of them suddenly stopped and stared.

For a horrible moment Ginger thought it was because something had happened to Mr Wong, but then he sat up next to her and stretched his arms.

'Mmmm,' he yawned. 'What time is it?'

Cerberus stretched and yawned too.

Ginger realised why the people were staring. They'd probably never seen a dog and human sleep-over before.

'Henry,' said Mrs Wong, hurrying forward. 'Thank God you're all right. I knew I should have come straight here after the vet's instead of spending all that time chasing those tjorkmin animals.'

Ginger stared at her.

'You knew this was where I was bringing Mr Wong?' she said.

Mrs Wong gave her a rueful smile.

'Everyone knew,' said an angry voice. 'Worst-kept secret of the century.'

Ginger saw that Mr Napier was struggling to get upright on his blackboard pointer. Ned gave him a hand. Ginger wished she had a blackboard pointer, too. She was feeling a bit faint.

'I'm fine, dear,' said Mr Wong to his wife, ignoring Mr Napier. 'I haven't had such a refreshing nap for ages. Thanks to Ginger and these other young members of my school family, I feel almost like my old self again. In fact, when I retire in a few years' time I'm thinking we might go skating in Norway.'

Mrs Wong beamed.

'Well, don't get too attached to any of these family members,' said Mr Napier, pointing to the dogs. 'As soon as I ring the appropriate authorities, these brutes won't be menacing our school community ever again.'

Ginger put her hand on Cerberus.

Mr Grosby stepped forward.

'I don't think you'll be ringing anybody,' he said to Mr Napier in his sternest School Council

President's voice. 'Except perhaps your lawyer. Locklan has told me about our dog biting poor Mr Wong. He also told me you knew about this and threatened to expel him if he told anyone else.'

'He's lying,' said Mr Napier.

'No,' said Mr Grosby. 'It seems you're the one who's been doing the lying. About Pets Day and the Education Department, for example.'

'Rubbish,' said Mr Napier, but Ginger could see fear in his eyes just like Ricebubble when she was accused of eating all the turkish delight and she realised she had icing sugar on her whiskers.

Dad stepped forward.

Ginger groaned. It was a noble thing for a teacher to try and defend his principal, but right now she couldn't bear it.

'You did something even worse than lying about stray dogs,' said Dad to Mr Napier. 'You said things to our daughter. About her and us. If you ever try and tell her again that she's not a precious part of our family, I'll come down on you so hard you'll poop yourself. Then I'll rub your nose in it.'

Ginger couldn't believe her ears. She'd never heard a teacher use such language.

Mr Napier was turning a scary shade of red.

'How dare you,' he hissed at Dad. 'You do not speak to a principal like that. I'm going to have you and your pathetic excuse for a family transferred so far away you'll need a compass to get there.'

Again, Ginger couldn't bear it.

Poor Mum and Dad, she thought miserably. You love this school more than anything. Do what you have to do. Apologise.

As Ginger had expected, Mum stepped forward. She put her face very close to Mr Napier's.

'Suspend us,' she said. 'Transfer us. Fire us. Drag us in front of a disciplinary committee. We don't care. Just don't ever, ever call our daughter trash again.'

Ginger stared, so many happy feelings bursting inside her she felt dizzy.

She saw Cerberus looking up at her.

One thing she did know, and she could see Cerberus knew too.

The tears running down her face weren't sneeze tears.

25

NINE LIVES

Ginger gave Cerberus a couple of minutes' privacy to say goodbye to the shed in the backyard. He'd only been back there a few nights, but she knew he'd appreciate it.

When he came out, she checked one more time that he really had to go.

'Are you sure?' she whispered in his ear.

His eyes told her he was.

Mum and Dad came and put their arms round her.

'We've talked about it,' said Mum, 'and if you like, Cerberus can stay. The cats won't like it but they'll just have to get used to it.'

Ginger could see the cats glaring out of the house. They didn't look as though they'd get used to having Cerberus around in a million years.

Poor things, she thought. It's hard enough for them getting used to me not handing out extra meals any more.

Ginger gave Mum and Dad a hug.

'Thanks,' she said sadly. 'But Cerberus has told me it's time for him to go.'

Ginger didn't ask Cerberus where he was going because she knew he'd show her.

She went with him along several streets.

They passed Ned and Isabel dropping RSPCA leaflets into mail boxes, advertising eight wonderful dogs for adoption.

'I'll be back to help you soon,' said Ginger. 'Once I've said goodbye to Cerberus.'

Ned and Isabel both gave Cerberus a hug, and Ginger could see how glad they were that they still had Roly and Fang.

A couple of streets further on, Ginger saw a person approaching with a dog on a lead.

It was Locklan with Fitzherbert.

'Dad says I can keep him,' said Locklan. 'As long as he sees a dog psychologist. We've found a really good one who specialises in dogs that bite school principals.'

Ginger smiled as she continued down the street with Cerberus. She'd known Fitzherbert was going to be OK since the day Locklan's dad came to the school to organise Mr Napier's resignation. He'd come in a new car. One without leather seats.

Many streets further on, Ginger couldn't contain herself any longer.

'Where are you going?' she asked Cerberus.

He didn't reply, just panted encouragingly, and a couple of minutes later he stopped outside a small house.

Ginger saw a car parked outside.

A familiar blue Corolla.

Mr Napier's car.

Then Ginger understood.

Somehow it was a tiny bit easier saying goodbye to Cerberus this way, knowing it was time for him to help an angry unhappy man without a family or friends or a job.

Ginger hugged Cerberus until he licked her face and she knew it was time to go.

'Goodbye,' she whispered. 'Thank you.'

Cerberus gave Ginger one final look, a look she knew she'd remember every day of her life.

Then Cerberus trotted up to Mr Napier's door and Ginger went home.

Later that week, after Ginger had helped deliver hundreds of RSPCA leaflets and had spoken to dozens of people in houses who were interested in adopting a stray dog, she found Ricebubble sitting on the mail box at home.

Ginger took a sneeze tablet. She didn't seem to need so many these days.

Then, slowly, she went over to Ricebubble.

'Don't be alarmed,' said Ginger. 'This is something I've been meaning to do since I saw your grandma's photo.'

Ricebubble saw that Ginger wasn't holding a cat-food box and gave a suspicious meow.

Ginger reached out and ran her hand slowly along Ricebubble's back.

Ricebubble looked alarmed, then puzzled.

Ginger was fascinated. Under the aristocratic coat of fluffy fur she could feel the outline of a skinny rat.

So it was true.

Cats were more like humans than Ginger had ever suspected.

Impressive on the outside, but fragile on the inside.

Amazing, thought Ginger. I'm standing here with my hand on a cat having a warm feeling. What's the world coming to?

Ricebubble seemed to be having a similar thought. She wasn't looking alarmed any more, or suspicious, and Ginger could have sworn she gave a surprised little purr.

Ginger decided not to let the moment go on too long, in case it got too much for Ricebubble.

She checked in the box for mail. There was one letter. It was to her, from the DNA laboratory.

Fuguggle, thought Ginger. The results of the test.

She started to open the envelope.

Then she stopped.

'Ginger,' sang out Mum from inside the house. 'Have you changed the kitty litter? When you've done that we're all going to watch a DVD. *Cats and Dogs*.'

'I'll do it now,' Ginger called.

She looked at the envelope again.

And sniffed the air.

All the familiar family smells were there. The soft tang of the carport cooling down in the evening air. The faint but exotic fragrance of Mum and Dad barbecuing dinner. The lovely minty aroma of a family that, if Ginger had her way, would start cleaning their teeth together any day now and telling each other jokes and laughing and spraying toothpaste around the bathroom.

Ginger smiled.

Then she tore the unopened letter into narrow kitty litter-sized strips.

'Scientific evidence can be useful,' Ginger said to Ricebubble, who was rubbing against her leg. 'But sometimes if you want to know the truth, you're better off just using your nose.'

Two Weeks with the Queen

A story of extraordinary power and poignancy. A heart-warming novel for young and old alike that has become an international bestseller, justly famed for its humour and emotion.

Totally Wicked!

Paul Jennings and Morris Gleitzman

A NOVEL IN SIX PARTS

It'll suck you in!

Something very weird is happening to Dawn and Rory. Slurping slobberers want to suck their bones out. Strange steel sheep want to smash them to pieces. Giant frogs want to crunch them up. Their parents can't help them. Dawn and Rory are on their own.

It's wild. It's wacky. It's TOTALLY WICKED!

Deadly!

Morris Gleitzman and Paul Jennings

A NOVEL IN SIX PARTS

You could die laughing!

Join Amy and Sprocket as they desperately search for their families – a quest that will take them to the weirdest nudist colony in the world. Uncovering deadly secret after deadly secret, Amy and Sprocket are lured deeper into a mystery that grows more exciting with every turn of the page.

Psst!
What's happening?

sneakpreviews@puffin

For all the inside information on the hottest new books,

click on the Puffin

www.puffin.co.uk

Read more in Puffin

For complete information about books available from Puffin – and Penguin – and how to order them, contact us at the appropriate address below. Please note that for copyright reasons the selection of books varies from country to country.

www.puffin.co.uk

In the United Kingdom: Please write to Dept EP, Penguin Books Ltd, Bath Road, Harmondsworth, West Drayton, Middlesex UB7 ODA

In the United States: Please write to Penguin Group (USA), Inc., P.O. Box 12289, Dept B, Newark, New Jersey 07101–5289 or call 1–800–788–6262

In Canada: Please write to Penguin Books Canada Ltd, 10 Alcorn Avenue, Suite 300, Toronto, Ontario M4V 3B2

In Australia: Please write to Penguin Books Australia Ltd, 250 Camberwell Road, Camberwell, Victoria 3124

In New Zealand: Please write to Penguin Books (NZ) Ltd, Private Bag 102902, North Shore Mail Centre, Auckland 10

In India: Please write to Penguin Books India Pvt Ltd, 11 Panscheel Shopping Centre, Panscheel Park, New Delhi 110 017

In the Netherlands: Please write to Penguin Books Netherlands bv, Postbus 3507, NL–1001 AH Amsterdam

In Germany: Please write to Penguin Books Deutschland GmbH, Metzlerstrasse 26, 60594 Frankfurt am Main

In Spain: Please write to Penguin Books S. A., Bravo Murillo 19, 1° B, 28015 Madrid

In Italy: Please write to Penguin Italia s.r.l., Via Felice Casati 20, I–20124 Milano

In France: Please write to Penguin France S. A., 17 rue Lejeune, F–31000 Toulouse

In Japan: Please write to Penguin Books Japan, Ishikiribashi Building, 2–5–4, Suido, Bunkyo-ku, Tokyo 112

In South Africa: Please write to Longman Penguin Southern Africa (Pty) Ltd, Private Bag X08, Bertsham 2013